CANADIAN SHORTS

A collection of Canadian-themed short
stories featuring top entries of the
2017 Canadian Shorts writing contest.

MISCHIEVOUS BOOKS

Canadian Shorts: A Collection of Short Stories

Copyright © 2017 Mischievous Books
mischievousbooks.com

Foreword, cover design & layout by Brenda Fisk
Stories Copyright © 2017 by the individual authors

ISBN: 978-0-9939823-9-2

PERMISSIONS

CONTENTS

FOREWORD

Words have always had the power to influence minds, to create communities and form nations. Our country was formed 150 years ago, with agreements of the mind and the stroke of a pen, entrenching written words into our Constitution. With those words, Canada became a nation, with cherished diversity, great privilege and responsibility.

Canadian authors create works that reflect the diversity of our country and, as writers, we too carry responsibility for the power of the written word.

Consider the impact of negatively charged words. How about hate, kill, or war? These single words carry significant threat, enough to constrict hearts, to raise blood pressures and close minds.

Now consider what happens with the inverse. Love, peace and hope invoke totally different emotions. Words matter. With words, we can sow destruction, or we can soothe hearts.

Many authors I know are generous with their knowledge and expertise. If you need information about something specific, there are many answers, freely offered, with nothing asked in return. Do you need input on a project? If so, you're likely to get experienced volunteers from writing groups and social networks. There is vast combined talent within our grasp. This collection celebrates the talent and generosity of authors, as well as our shared desire to be a positive influence.

As citizens of Canada, a country of inclusion and well-being, I feel we have a responsibility to help those in need. As authors, we are observers of life and are connected to emotions and experiences outside our own. It's what enables us to write from our hearts. Because of this connection, many authors are especially impacted by humanitarian crises. Some say there is no time for compassion, that it has no place in our world any more, that it only makes us weak. I think this is a grave error. Compassion is not a sign of weakness. It requires strength of character, but is meaningless without action.

Like the effect of a single word, we as individuals can have an influence. We can take action. As a group, could we have greater impact? Could we help change lives, if not on a global scale, perhaps in our own country, in our communities?

One timely issue is the crisis in the Middle East, which has culminated in thousands of people being forced to flee their homelands, families divided, children torn from their parents. Many are housed in refugee centres, waiting to come to Canada. They have hopes for a better future, for safety, community, and opportunity. What if we could help them?

Our Prime Minister Justin Trudeau recently sent a very clear message of Canada's welcome to other nations, especially those currently in turmoil, fleeing war and seeking asylum from persecution. Sure, government agencies assist, but there is still greater need. That's why some Canadian families and small organizations have taken it upon themselves to help in their own ways. They are joining with others to raise donations, to form support groups, to sponsor entire families. Small cash donations may seem inconsequential but, when combined, make a real impact.

We can help too. When planning the Canadian Shorts writing contest, I wanted to create something better than just another contest. I wanted to use the power of many authors to create a uniquely Canadian book and donate proceeds. Volunteer time has contributed to the design, layout, judging, organizing, and promotion of this project. Each sale of this book generates a few dollars in royalties. When added together, well, who knows what we can achieve?

All proceeds from this project will be donated to The Canadian Council for Refugees, "a non profit umbrella organization committed to the rights and protection of refugees in Canada and around the world and to the settlement of refugees and immigrants in Canada.[1]" Organizations such as this have been crucial during recent humanitarian catastrophes.

I'm proud Canada is an accepting nation that encourages individual and cultural diversity. I am so pleased to promote great Canadian authors represented in this work: Canadian Shorts, a collection of the contest's top short stories of 2017. I hope you enjoy reading them.

Brenda Fisk
Managing Editor
Mischievous Books, Calgary, AB

[1] Canadian Council for Refugees http://ccrweb.ca/en/about-ccr

FAR OUT ON THE SAGEBRUSH SEA
by Donna Quick

There was a full moon last night. I could see it shining on the ocean from my window in the seniors' high-rise. But moonlight at the coast isn't like the full moons of my prairie childhood; there was no power to its brightness. The waves tried to shrug it off, and it was broken up and restless.

It was nothing like the moon shining down on a silvery sea of grass so bright that you thought your heart would burst with the beauty of it, a shimmering world that stretched on forever until it met the velvety-purple bowl of the sky clamped down on the horizon.

I've never seen two people so affected by the moon as Sandra and Scott, and this is their story, but I've felt the power of the moon too. I had no trouble saying no to Harold Miller all through grade 11. But that summer night when we'd been parked at the edge of town, it just seemed the most natural thing to step out on the prairie and do what Harold and the moon were urging me to do. And once that was over and done with, there didn't seem to be much point in saying no to Frank Bauer the next winter, which is how I ended up married with two kids by the time I was 21.

Scott and Sandra and I grew up living side by side on a big shelf of prairie that ran alongside the South Saskatchewan River. Sandra was an only child, so as soon as she was old

1

enough to scramble off the water trough onto the back of her fat little Shetland, she started riding over to spend her free time with me. About the age when she was too old to enjoy dressing up little pigs in doll clothes and pushing them around the barnyard in a baby buggy, she'd graduated to an old, gentle cow pony. That pony never took a wrong step as long as he was packing Sandra around. I guess he didn't want to take a chance on having to go back to his old job of chasing cows. Once Sandra could get around a little faster and cover more ground, she started going over to Scott's ranch instead so she'd have someone to ride with. Since my dad was more of a farmer than a rancher, we only had big, slow workhorses, so there was no way I could keep up with her.

It was hard to know when playing together became dating, but by grade 8 people thought of Sandra and Scott as a couple. They even looked something alike, although Scott's hair was the colour of a cornstalk after the first hard frost and Sandra's hair had just a little red mixed in with the gold. They seemed to find no end of things to do together, but what I remember best took place on the two or three nights each month in the summer when the moon was at its fullest.

On those special nights, it would be just as bright as day out on the prairie. Everywhere would be the sharp, tangy smell of the sage, with the air so still you could almost hear the moonlight beaming down. There would be a few crickets softly chirping, and maybe off in the distance a cow bawling to her calf. Sometimes you could hear a far-off train sounding its faint, lonely whistle. But somehow those noises just made the prairie seem more empty and more quiet, and then you'd hear Sandra and Scott.

You could usually see them moving slowly across the shining silver plain just before you heard them. Sandra was riding a pretty little part Thoroughbred mare by then. Scott had bought the first purebred Quarter Horse to be seen in our part of the country, a palomino with a golden sheen to her coat. Even from far off in the distance, the moon would glint on those glossy horsehides and the two blond heads that were so close together. Everything would be flooded by that pure, clear light, and you could see Sandra and Scott holding hands as they rode along side by side.

Other times you'd hear them singing before you saw them. They sang all those old-time Western classics like Ghost Riders in the Sky and Cattle Call and a whole bunch of songs that were all about moonlight. They'd slowly pass by just to the east of our house, their shadows growing longer and longer as they rode away. It was a sight and a sound that you'd never forget for the rest of your life. And whenever you saw a full moon, no matter where you might be living, you felt that something had been left behind back there on the prairie that you'd never find again.

Everybody expected the two of them to get married right after high school. I can still remember Sandra coming up to me at the Christmas dance in the community hall, her eyes shining with happiness. She held up her left hand and showed me the ring on her finger made from a bent horseshoe nail. "This will have to do for now," she said, "but Scott will buy me a real ring after he sells his calves in the fall."

But partway through grade 12, Sandra's mother started carrying on about how she had been putting money aside every month, no matter how low cattle prices were, so Sandra could go to university and get her teaching certificate. And being a dutiful daughter, Sandra went off to the U of A in Edmonton the next September.

She rode over to see me just before she left. Her horse nibbled at the straggly tufts of grass in the barnyard while she stood holding the reins and talking to me. "I don't want to go, Wanda. I'll miss Scott so much. But after all the things my mother did without to pay for my education, I just can't disappoint her and stay home until Scott saves up enough for us to get married."

Scott was pretty cut up about it at first. I remember him asking: "Why would she do this to me? I thought all she ever wanted was to be a ranch wife." I told him just to be patient, that she'd probably be homesick and quit after the first semester.

Then just before Sandra was due home for her first visit at Christmas, Scott had a big fight with his daddy about how their new bull should be a Charolais instead of another Hereford. There were so many hard feelings afterward that he decided he'd enlist and serve one hitch in the army while he was waiting for Sandra to come back.

But people sometimes change when they leave home for the first time. Before Sandra came back for the summer holidays, Scott received a Dear John letter. It just seemed logical to sign up again and give his heart an extra couple of years to heal before he headed back to the ranch.

Sandra came to visit me as soon as she got back home. By then I was married to Frank, living in town and expecting my first baby at Christmas.

"I feel just awful about Scott," she told me. "But, Wanda, you can't imagine what it's like to be with people who don't spend all their time talking about crops and cattle prices. There's a whole other world out there, with fancy restaurants and stores that don't just carry clothes our mothers would wear and dances where there's never any loud country music."

I tried to understand, but all I could think about was the way Scott looked so sad and haunted the last time I saw him.

By the time Scott finally got back to the ranch, everything had changed. His younger brother, Hugh, was riding a green three-year-old across a dry creek bed one day when it probably spooked at a snake sunning itself on a stone. His head was all bashed in by the rocks, and he was dead when they found him the next day. Scott's dad started drinking right after that, and he made a bunch of bad decisions when it came to buying and selling.

Even before Scott came home, the bank had foreclosed. His mother had gone to live with one of his married sisters, and his father had moved into the single men's residence run by the Salvation Army.

The new owner of the ranch said there would always be a job for a good hand like Scott. So not knowing what else to do, he moved into the bunkhouse.

About that same time, we got word that Sandra had married a petroleum engineer she met at the university. She ended up living in far-flung spots all over the world, wherever the oil business was booming. Her mother suddenly looked about 10 years older. I'm sure her plans hadn't included a daughter she hardly ever saw, not to mention the grandchildren once they started arriving.

It wasn't long before Scott started driving into town almost every night to spend his evenings at one or another of the hotel bars. Pretty soon he ran into Beverly Seitz, who'd been in his classes all through high school. As long as Sandra had been around, she never did anything more than say "Hi" to Scott.

I met Beverly in Woolworth's one day soon after Scott came home. We'd never been friends, but this time she walked right over to me. "Is it really true that Sandra got married and won't be coming back?" she asked. "I always thought she and Scott were a sure thing."

It wasn't hard to guess where Beverly's thoughts were heading. Don't get your hopes up, I can remember thinking. Beverly was no match for Sandra. She was shorter and already thicker around the waist, with drab brown hair that she wore in a tight ponytail to hide her natural frizz.

But I didn't take into consideration how lonely it must be out on the ranch with no family around. Beverly set her sights on Scott and just kept chasing until she wore him down. She made sure that Scott Jr. was on the way before she suggested they get married.

Of course the bunkhouse was no place for a family.

Scott sold his saddle, his palomino mare and the two colts she had raised and moved into town. He was able to get a job at the feed mill right off, but you never saw a more miserable looking man. When I ran into him at the post office one day, he said: "You know, Wanda, I always expected to spend all my days on the back of a horse looking after my own cows on my own land. What the hell went wrong?" It was a pretty sad adjustment, and I didn't have any answers for him this time.

Except for Christmas cards, none of us heard anything of Sandra until the year she came back to town for her father's funeral. I met her at the airport, and I was the only one to see how well she was taking it and how she was able to be such a comfort to her mother.

At the funeral, we bumped into Scott on the steps of the church. "Hello, Scott," I heard her say softly. He went as white as one of those newborn Charolais calves he never did get to raise, and Sandra didn't look much better. I don't know what else she said, but they disappeared behind the church for quite a few minutes. By the time she took her place inside, the tears were streaming down her face. Everybody said how it was nice to see a daughter who loved her daddy as much as she had, and didn't they wish they could say the same for their own children.

Once Sandra left town and went back to her family, Scott started hitting the bottle just like his father had, and every year he got a little worse. The feed mill was no place for somebody to be making mistakes around all that complicated machinery, but they kept him on until he was able to retire with half a pension. He picked up a few days' work at the auction mart now and then and tried to stay sober until after the weekly cattle sale. Beverly had seen the writing on the wall a few years earlier. She went back to the beauty parlour where she worked right after high school, even though there were three kids to look after by then

The years rolled along, and there wasn't much news of

Sandra except for those Christmas cards. So we were all shocked to suddenly hear that she had divorced her husband and was moving back to be near her mother, who by this time was in a nursing home in town. She bought one of those smart new condos they built next to the golf course. Just to keep herself busy, she started taking a few courses to upgrade her teaching credentials, now that we finally had a local college.

I don't know when she and Scott met up again. All I know is that pretty soon he started coming around to Sandra's apartment on a regular basis, married or not. By all reports, Beverly was hardly talking to Scott by then. He was still the best looking man of his age in the county. Sandra hadn't lost any of her looks either, although her red-gold hair was just a little darker now. Beverly, who knew all about such things, was quick to say to anybody who would listen, "Clairol Autumn Haze, straight out of the bottle."

Scott always brought along a jug of wine or a case of beer on his visits. I don't think Sandra had ever been much of a drinker, but by the end of that first winter, they were pretty evenly matched drinking buddies. When the hot weather came, you could often hear snatches of those old cowboy songs floating through the open patio doors of Sandra's apartment. Pretty soon Sandra's daughter Lois, who lived in the East, got word of the way her mother was carrying on and decided to come and see for herself. How someone as open and friendly as Sandra could raise a daughter who was so stiff and uptight I don't know. Lois sure didn't think much of any of us.

I was the only one besides Lois who was there the night it happened. I had dropped in after supper to ask if Sandra would like to join the church choir, and Scott was already on the sofa, working his way through a bottle of rye. You could tell that Lois was less than thrilled to have him there, but there was no way she was going to go off and leave the two of them alone.

It was just an ordinary evening until the clouds suddenly drifted apart and we realized there was a full moon that night. We'd moved out on the balcony by then, and suddenly the big expanse of lawn all around the condos lit up almost like the prairie of our childhoods.

Sandra looked at Scott, and Scott looked at Sandra, and then he said: "Well, I figure it's about time to saddle up and ride out towards the river. Want to come along?"

By this time they'd both had three or four stiff drinks, and Lois was horrified. "Don't be crazy! You'll drive yourself into the ditch. And everybody will be able to see the two of you together because of the moonlight."

She did her best to talk them out of it, but finally Sandra just picked up her keys and they walked out to her car.

That was the last time anybody ever saw either of them. Lois gave them a little leeway and didn't report her mother missing until early afternoon of the next day. Beverly turned up at the police station not too long afterward.

The search party found Sandra's car parked not too far from the river, a mile or so from her old home. There were all kinds of places along the river where the bank was undercut, and lots of spots where it looked like a person or a cow might have gone over the edge. Some of the searchers climbed down and walked right next to the river for miles on either side, but there was nothing to be seen.

Sandra's daughter carried on something awful. "I should have been able to stop them! I knew I should have stopped them!" she kept saying. Finally she had to go back East, and that was the last we heard from her.

All through the summer, people kept checking the sandbar in the bend of the river where dead cows and horses always wash up after a hard winter, but it never did any good.

Beverly hung around until the insurance was settled, which took a while on account of there being no bodies. But then she left town, and we heard that she had opened up a beauty parlour in Calgary.

I suppose I should have said something while Lois was still in town, since I'm the only one who knows what happened to them that night. But I'm sure she wouldn't have believed me, and no one else would have either.

You see, I know what took place that last night just as surely as if I'd been an old coyote sitting out on the prairie getting set to howl at the moon.

They would have walked along hand in hand, their footsteps hushed by the gleaming softness of the grass stretching ahead of them as far as they could see. Their shadows would be patches of dusky black velvet silently following them across the molten plain.

The scent of the sage they crushed underfoot would rise up to meet them. Off in the distance they'd hear the faint echo of a train whistle, but nothing else would disturb the stillness.

Then at a certain point where the moonbeams seemed to shine down extra brightly, they'd pass between them and just walk off the face of the earth as we know it. They'd be in another time and another place, but the moon would still be with them. And this time it would be the way it was meant to be, and they'd never be apart again.

At least that's what I like to tell myself..

AFTER THE CHANGE
by Maureen O'Hare

Gone. Everyone is gone. Buildings loom over me as I walk down the deserted street. Cars covered in dust line the roadway, doors open, trunks agape, testimony to survivors scavenging long ago. It's hard to believe I once lived here, in Red Stone, Alberta, back when the world was normal.

Well, that's what my parents call it, as if having cell phones and cars and all that stuff everyone had was normal. How things are now, that's normal, at least to my friends and me. Maybe that's why so many grown-ups go nuts or run off or whatever they do. Even in our settlement, most families have been affected. Sarah's mom disappeared into the desert and never came back. Edric's uncle jumped off a cliff. I dunno, could it be something that happens when you get old, like thirty? Can't they handle how the world has changed?

What this insignificant Canadian town must have been like back then, cars and trucks racing so fast, and people everywhere? I don't remember much from that time; it's more of a dream, or a nightmare. The candy store on the corner, my mom and I went there once when I was little. That world is never coming back, no matter what the oldies say. Is there even a country called Canada anymore? Most of the towns are empty, mom says, with people living in small groups. It's easier to forage if your group isn't too

11

big.

The street is silent. Nothing moves, except the aurora streaking across the sky. Mom said there used to be stars. Now, bright colours flash and streamers of light arc in a constant rainbow. Solar flares cause the kaleidoscope in the atmosphere and at least it's pretty.

Mom hates when I scavenge or hunt alone. She might ban me from going out if she catches me. Game is scarce at this time of the year but hopefully I can find something the reavers missed.

Mom doesn't understand. I'm different from the others at our camp. I don't fit in, except with Kieran and Emily, my only friends. The other kids are just so dumb. They think I'm weird because I know stuff. My mom's a librarian, for Stellar's sake, of course I know everything. I'll show 'em. I'm gonna find something nobody else found. I'm gonna come home a hero.

Broken glass tinkles to my left. I squint into the harsh sun, Winchester rifle pressed to my shoulder. A Goliath roach, at least twenty centimeters across, emerges from under rusted junk. The brown insect's long antennae twitch and its segmented exoskeleton glints in the light.

Skreeeek!

The pile shifts under the enormous bug's weight as its carapace scrapes along the metal. My skin prickles in disgust when it skitters under an abandoned car. I hate Goliaths. I aim into the shadows. I'll shoot it if I can but the roach doesn't show itself again. Lots of creatures are different since the flares began. Could it be growing smarter instead of just bigger? Will we have giant, intelligent roaches soon? An icy shiver trickles down my spine. I hate Goliaths.

Bang! Crash!

Noises echo around the corner. I creep forward, my finger on the trigger toward an alley, cloaked in darkness, rubble from the adjacent building obscuring the entrance.

Crash! Craaack! Screeee!

I speed up, wary for traps. Ahead, more Goliaths, roil across chunks of plaster wall. Something must be down there. I sight down the length of my rifle. Every shot must count.

Crack! One roach's guts spray against the wall.

Crack! Crack! Two more splatter.

The remaining insects chitter and attack their slain brethren. There are so many. I clang my rifle's butt against a corroded steel fender and dust billows up from the surface. The surviving insects look up from their meals and scatter into the darkness of the ruined buildings. Coughing, I wave the dust away from my face.

What brought the Goliaths to this place? Is it something I can bring home for dinner? A rabbit? Why would they attack in such numbers?

A deep growl resonates as I sneak closer and my heart thumps uncontrollably. I swallow to keep my fear in check.

"Fear is good, fear keeps you alert, fear keeps you alive," I repeat aloud the safety mantra taught to me by the Captain. The rumble continues.

Why am I not walking away? Running? My brain screams at me but I keep moving toward the pile of debris. My heart booms in my ears, my breath stutters between my teeth. What am I doing? I find myself shoving rubble and boards away, my rifle falling to the ground beside me.

What am I doing? This isn't safe. Still the rumble deepens. Run! Sweat pours down my neck, clammy and cold.

Chucking the last board away, green glowing eyes and a large furry body reveal themselves. I scream and jump back, scrambling towards my Winchester. Before reaching it, I again feel compelled to move forward. A deep throaty rumble erupts from the creature, sounding less like a growl and more like... purring?

My head throbs to the same tempo. As I step, my hand strays to the hilt of my knife in its sheath. Looking closer, I see it's a cat. Not just a regular cat, but one of the Changed ones that began appearing a few years after the collapse, a huge tabby striped beast weighing at least twenty-five kilograms.

I try to pull my knife from the sheath but stop as the rumbling, purring gets louder. Reaching forward, I touch the cat. Why? What am I doing? What's happening to me? The animal is dusty and dirty. Pain streaks through its back leg. How can I feel this? I look closer seeing the misshapen limb with blood seeping and white bone peeking through. Other nicks and cuts mar the animal's coat.

:Help?:

Where is this coming from? I look around but there is no one speaking. No voice, instead something heard in my head. I reach out a trembling hand, pull it back.

"Help you?" My voice is barely a whisper.

The cat nods. An image forms in my head, a human, looking remarkably like me, carrying this enormous cat in my arms. My brain gibbers at the visions racing through it, somehow projected to me by the rhythmic purring, the cat jumping, the ledge coming loose, falling. Pain lances through me at the leg-breaking impact, the cat dragging itself under the debris while the roaches scent blood and attack, and finally, my shots killing the Goliaths.

Am I reading the cat's mind? That's absurd. Could it be the cat? Projecting these images? The purring intensifies with a plaintive meow.

:Leave?:

I must help this strange animal. The need overwhelms me. Why? Carapace scraping against stone returns me to reality. The roaches are returning, emboldened by the stench of blood and carrion.

"I'm gonna pick you up, cat. You better not bite me or this will be one very short rescue." My hands shake when I reach under the beast.

I hope it can understand me 'cause those paws are really big and they are going to be close to my face. I grunt under the impressive weight of the tabby and it holds completely still, purring louder.

Leveling my rifle one-handed at the boldest of the roaches, I shoot and miss. Legs ticking and scratching, the other bugs skitter into the darkness, leaving an escape route.

I reposition my grip under the ever-increasing weight and a faint whimper emerges from the cat. Pain shoots through me. I need to splint this broken leg. My skull throbs with each step.

:Turn:

I feel the instruction in my head, an image superimposed over my vision showing me where to go. The direction is as good as any, so I comply.

Can you read my mind? I think at the cat. Nothing.

:Keep going:

An image of a path flashes. Again I comply, and we arrive at a doorway. I peer inside. The room is strewn with junk from The Before, no roaches or reavers.

:Here:

There's a tiny corner room, it must have been an office or storage room. I kneel with a groan, resting the cat on the blankets. A small mewl of pain tears free. Rummaging through my daypack I pull out first aid supplies.

"I can help you, cat, but it's gonna take time. I'm going to grab the stuff so I can splint your leg," I explain. The cat purrs but doesn't respond. Hoping it understands, I get up and haul my rifle along, just in case. I need wood for a splint and a fire. It gets cold at night and somehow I don't think I'm going to get home before sunset.

I backtrack to the main room and begin my search. Shelves stand in rows along the length of the shop. Some are toppled, and boxes and crates are also strewn about. As I wander, I find a door along the back wall of the building. It's not very noticeable, painted the same colour as the walls. Only the metal handle distinguishes it. Locked.

I want to explore but I'll do that later. My wounded cat comes first. My cat? When did I start thinking of the beast as mine? I drag the supplies back to the animal. It looks up at me and blinks its bright green eyes. I suddenly know it's a him

:Hurts:

"I know. I can help but it's going to hurt even more before it feels better. I'll do my best to treat your injuries." I busy myself building a small fire, gathering my medical kit to dull the pain I feel coursing through the injured cat's leg.

:Trust:

Sensing his voice in my head no longer feels scary. It's comforting, as though it's always been there. My headache has disappeared.

"Why?" I ask.

:Not know, trust:

A disconcerting feeling accompanies this thought. It seems the cat is as bewildered by this as I am.

"Ok then, lets get to it. This is gonna hurt". Pulling on the fractured leg until I feel a click, the pain in my mind recedes. The break is aligned. I'm amazed when he doesn't move as I manipulate his injuries. He merely purrs that deep rumble, louder and louder, not moving an inch. Splint applied, I sew the wound closed after dusting it with the powder our camp medic makes from moldy bread and lemon rinds. It sounds icky but it works.

:Gratitude:

I stroke between his ears, an impulsive gesture, but he bumps his head against my hand. I feel his pleasure in the touch and continue to stroke his massive head. His purr rumbles through my head and hand. Strangely, I feel better, calmer, and happier. I think the cat does too.

:Sleep: The cat sighs and closes his eyes.

"Since there is no way to make it back home before dark. I'm going to look around and set up barricades in case anyone, or anything, comes looking for a meal." I think really hard to project an image of Goliaths at the cat. He doesn't move, just purrs that rumbly sound. I scour the dimming room, finding and piling up items as a defensive fortification against anyone trying to enter. I trip, tumbling into a shelf with a crash.

:Hurt? Monsters?:

Goliaths and other creatures appear in my head. I think an image of my fall to the cat and hear - feel - a snort of mirth. Maybe he can read my mind?

Once the barricade is ready, I make a final sweep of the shop. As I pass the counter I notice something metal gleaming underneath and fish out a set of keys. Maybe they unlock that secret door. Tossing these relics of another age in my daypack, I return to the cat, his green eyes glowing in the dimness.

* * *

The travel rations every hunter takes when they leave camp come in useful. I don't want to leave the cat to hunt. I pull a small metal pot to heat water, adding my store of dried meat and vegetables from my pack. I crumble some way-bread into it once it's ready. This extends the small amount of food to satisfy two hungry creatures and the hard, twice-baked bread is far more palatable when soaked in the savoury meat broth. The cat sniffs the mixture, shared into two portions.

"Careful it's still hot. Wait a minute, until it cools a bit more".

The cat patiently licks his chops but waits until I test the stew and declare it cool enough to eat. He daintily eats his share and licks the pot clean. I use my fingers to grab the last bits from my bowl, an old-time plastic container from travel rations. I have two more pieces of way-bread and some tea. We can share it for breakfast.

"What should I call you? I can't just call you cat." An overlay in my vision of the cat moving sinuously among trees, stripes blending nearly unseen into the underbrush.

"How 'bout I call you Orion? It's a constellation in the

sky, named for a famous hunter in ancient times". The cat preens and projects images of his hunting prowess.

"Exactly!" I reply. The cat, now apparently named, purrs and bumps my hand.

"Where is your family?" Flash, Orion, huge in comparison, playing with his littermates. Another burst, a human in a white coat with a huge needle, a second human in black grabbing a cat by the scruff. Running, fear, loss. Horror and sadness strike me, I sob and hug the giant cat.

:Hurt inside:

Recognition seizes me. Those humans look like a doctor or scientist and a man in uniform with a maple leaf on his lapel.

"Oh Orion! I'm so sorry. Are they all gone?" I run my fingers through his soft coat.

:Gone, all gone: An image of a tiny still body, soft coat matted by blood.

Orion growls a deep throaty sound. His tail lashes back and forth the fur on it standing on end his anger obvious. :Kill:

A flash of hatred so intense I feel sick and have to force down the gorge rising in my throat.

:Evil men: Orion hisses and snarls a sound so malevolent I shudder.

"Oh Orion, We will get revenge. These fiends", I spit out the word, "can't get away with this".

Somehow I have joined forces with the cat. I have no idea how we will do this, I only know we must try. The hair on my arms lifts and I wish I had a tail I could lash like Orion's. I lean back against the wall and the cat carefully shifts his weight until his body is inclined against me. His head on my thighs is in easy reach for my stroking fingers, the rhythmic motion soothing our anger.

Crash!

I awake to the sounds of someone entering, and my barricade hits the floor. Orion and I leap our feet. Reavers!

Three grimy men push through the shop door, blocked

with junk, one carrying a gun I recognize. It's Edric Levenson's, the only Tavor Carbine in our whole encampment. One of the men is limping. Maybe Edric got a few good licks before they got him. Just as I glance at the cat, one of the bandits sweeps into Orion's tiny stockroom lair. Startled, he jumps back.

Snarling and swiping his huge claws, Orion distracts the man. I raise my rifle to snap off a quick shot. It hits him in the shoulder, spinning him into the junk strewn shelves. The other reavers duck and cover their weapons. I can hear moans of pain as Orion and I dodge away. We can't escape. They control the only exit.

Orion meows. .:Idea: The hidden door flashes across my vision.

"It's worth a try!" Shooting blindly to keep the raiders heads down, the limping cat and I crawl toward our only chance to escape.

"Joe, go after them. It's just her and one of them 'bominations. We can get 'em, easy," screeches the reaver I shot.

"Screw you, I ain't gettin' shot up!" Joe yells back. "I'm staying right here. "

Peering around a corner, we see the wounded bandit crawl gracelessly towards the others. He shoves the youngest brigand and growls an order to find us. The bandit nods, grasps his rifle, and skulks through the store.

The cat hops awkwardly to keep his splinted leg up off the floor. The unwieldy length of the splint collides with debris. Hearing the noise, the young reaver turns, running hell-bent for our position. He is on us before I can get my gun up, and kicks me, his steel-toed boot catching me in the ribs. My rifle spins out of my grasp. His boot winds up for another kick, this one aimed at my head.

Orion lets out an ear-shattering shriek, a sound unlike anything I have ever heard from a cat. He jumps towards the attacking bandit, splinted leg hardly hindering his leap. Claws rake the reaver's face and he jumps away. Blood spurts. This reaver is really just a kid, not really much older than me. I steel myself, fear giving me strength.

An image superimposes over my vision. I nod and pull my knife, darting a feint at the reaver's mangled face. He kicks out, raising Edric's carbine straight at my chest. The cat jumps again, his claws adhering onto the brigand's back, teeth sinking into his neck. The gun explodes and a bullet collides with the wall. Bits of brick embed in my cheek.

Crap! That shot would have killed me if not for Orion. The kid screams and vainly tries to pull off the shrieking feline. While he is distracted I plunge my knife deep into his chest. He groans and falls, Orion hopping from the raiders body as it topples face down. We race to the secret door before the other two reavers can reach us.

I hear them yelling for the kid. "Hey kid, you get 'em?" The guy named Joe swears when there is no answer and I can hear him start toward the back of the store. He sprays bullets from his semi-auto for cover.

Finally reaching the secret door, I try desperately to find the right key. Oh god, what if none of them fit? My hands shake so badly I fumble and drop the ring. Sweat breaks out on my neck, terror makes my heart pound and my breath pant. I wince, waiting for a rain of bullets.

Orion growls and an image of the reaver coming down the aisle next to us flashes in my head. I redouble my efforts and finally a key fits the lock. Twisting, I pull the door open. Slamming it closed behind us, I jam a length of wood through the handle. This should hold the door for a while.

A shadow blocks the light under the door. I raise the carbine, aiming above the handle. The gun clicks. My heart stops.

CRAAASHHH!! The door slams open and the bandit appears in the opening, an evil smile transfixing his face. I grope beside me for the rifle, struggling to bring the muzzle up before he reaches me. I can see blood staining his shoulder courtesy of my earlier shot.

A blood-curdling roar emanates from the cat. Orion jumps, landing with claws extended, slashing and ripping. He bites the marauder's ear and neck but the man manages to dislodge him, throwing him to the ground. The cat shrieks in pain but launches himself again. This time he lands on the man's back, unbalancing him. The bandit falls forward, striking the wall. I hear a dull crack and the outlaw goes limp. Orion snarls a victory cry.

Shaking, with tears running down my face, I crawl towards the cat. Orion just saved me, twice. "Are you ok? Were you hurt?" I run my hands along the cat's soft fur searching for injury.

:Fine. No more hurt:

Relief floods through me, "C'mon, we have to get out of here". Orion grabs the daypack I had abandoned as we entered. It catches on something and I reach over to dislodge it from a metal ring set into the floor. Brushing debris away, a thin line materializes. It's barely noticeable but I'm certain it's a trap door. Tugging on the ring, the trap door opens easily. Orion pokes his head into the opening and a dim room appears in my head.

"Is anyone down there"?

Orion shakes his head. :Long time ago. Not now: The cat listens intently. :Bad one comes:

An image of the reaver, using his rifle as a crutch. He's coming.

Around us there are boxes, hundreds of them. I look into a couple and find shotgun shells and bullets. Others contain cans of food and dry staples like spaghetti, rice and oats. I think there are even some medicines, but I'm not sure. This must have been a black market shop during the collapse. I knew Red Stone was one of the last communities in Alberta to collapse when the flares came. These provisions are priceless. Maybe I won't be grounded forever. With all this stuff, I shouldn't even get in trouble for going out on my own. We find a door blocked with heavy brace. I lift the wood and the door swings open into a tunnel of some kind.

I grab a few choice items to show the captain and my mom when we get back. Yanking the door closed we trudge down the murky passageway.

"C'mon Orion," I grunt as I lift his weight along with my pack. "I hope that thug doesn't find this place. There is so much stuff here that could help our whole camp. We'd better get away. More reavers will come.

The walls of the tunnel are dirt, the earth dry and hard. It's dark but I can make out the walls and ground ahead of me. I can see old wooden posts and beams periodically propped up to provide support for the structure. The tunnel is straight and long. It looks as though it has been here for hundreds of years. Maybe its part of an old mine like our encampment. Mom said they mined for coal around here around a hundred and fifty years ago. After what seems like hours I see a gradual brightening, so slow I didn't notice it until I realize I can see the colour of Orion's coat and make out signs with arrows attached to the support beams. I hope these arrows point to the exit.

Stumbling on the uneven ground, I fall forward catching myself on a support beam, dislodging it. Rocks and dirt rain down on my head. The stream of stone becomes a downpour. An image of a running cat flashes in my head but my feet are already moving. Rocks continue to fall, a fist-sized one hammers against the left size of my head, I trip, scrambling to regain my feet and keep moving.

Coughing and choking I emerge into the night. Orion shakes his head and sneezes. Looking back I can see the entrance is now blocked by rubble. The aurora of light illuminates the landscape with twisting patterns. Head throbbing and blood trickling from my temple we trek through the desert towards home. What am I going to tell mom about my new friend? She doesn't even like cats.

THE CURE
by Michele Lisiecki

Running for the Cure in Calgary had never been on my radar before, yet here I was panting along with the rest of those who'd been touched by the disease that knew no bounds.

The grey clouds blocked out any hope of the sun burning away the spring chill. I pushed my legs harder, zig zagged between the bodies as I disappeared among them. I was as invisible to them as they were to me. Just like my son's father. What was his name again? A drunken one night stand--my mother loved that--but it gifted me my son.

A tall, thin man with brown hair greying at the temples stumbled in front of me and I had to leap out of the way to avoid running into him. I glanced over my shoulder to see the man right himself and a cold grip squeezed my stomach. Oh God. Oh God not-

I stared straight ahead, not seeing anything or anyone, running on automatic, as the face of the man responsible for my son's death hung before me. I crossed the finish line, slowed to a walk as my pulse hammered in my throat.

I needed to get out of here before he crossed the line. He'd seen me, I knew that for sure. He'd want to find me and try to say words of encouragement, because that's what doctors were trained to do.

A hand gripped my arm and I yanked free of it. A

blond, petite woman with wide brown eyes and furrowed brows stared back at me. "You okay?"

Oh—Tori.

I sighed and gave a quick nod. I had met Tori after Brady died. She joined the grief counselling group I attended after her mother lost her battle with cancer. I don't know how I would have survived without her friendship and unwavering support. I certainly wouldn't be here running.

"You did it Jen," Tori said, patient and sympathetic as always. "Brady would be so proud of you."

How do you know what my son would be proud of, I wanted to say, he's dead. Instead, I took in a shallow breath and gave a half smile. Sometimes it was hard to be grateful.

"You made good time. You must have been just behind me." Tori's face had no sweat on it and she held a half-eaten apple in her hand. "Let's go get some fruit and water. You must be hungry."

I followed behind Tori as she blazed a trail through the sea of pink t-shirts. Her strong body was built for running where as my too thin limbs hung awkwardly from my torso as though they were built for sorrow. Someone brushed past me and I had to grab the side of a table full of boxes of bananas to regain my balance. Two years of going back and forth to the hospital and another of grieving had left me weak. I don't know if I even trusted my own body anymore after what I saw happen to my boy.

It was difficult to remember Brady sometimes, the way he was before the illness. I tried to hang on to the good memories. Happier times when there was laughter, playing with friends, his cheeks a healthy glow, but the intensity of antiseptic, vomit and the stench of pending death always stole them away.

Tori shoved the cold bottle into my hand and I almost dropped it. I shook my head to clear out the confusion that seemed to be my new normal. I turned the cap and drank even though I didn't feel thirsty. People packed themselves around the tables of yogurt, fruit and drinks as panic gripped my mind. I wanted to claw my way out of the crowds.

Tori yanked me toward a small crowd of people. "I don't believe it. Oh my God," Tori said over and over again as she dragged me behind her. She said over her shoulder, "I have to say hello to an old friend. You are going to love him."

I didn't think I'd love him at all, but I couldn't get the words out. A tall man and woman stood with their backs to us, each with a little blond girl in their arms. They would be about Brady's age before he…well, he'd be older now but I couldn't seem to image him as any age but his last. The wheezing breeze pushed past me as I stared ahead at our target. I just needed to get through this meet and greet, let Tori say her hellos and I could go home. I'd like to think I had a good book waiting for me or some cleaning to do or another project, but I knew I'd likely do what I did every day. Sit at the kitchen table and stare at the swing set in the back yard or walk by his closed bedroom door and sit on the floor leaning up against it. If I really felt adventurous I'd open it and stare at its contents, now layered with a thick film of dust.

Tori stopped and I almost bumped into her. She tapped the man's shoulder while the blond girl watched over the other and she said, "Jake?" The man turned his head as his child adjusted her position from her perch in this arms and his face spread into a smile.

I blinked.

They hugged and his attention turned to me as he said, "Hello Ms. Artfield. I thought I saw you earlier. How are you?"

Again, I blinked.

"You know each other? You never said, Jen." She rubbed my arm with a big, sloppy grin on her face.

Still I could do nothing but blink.

"I was Brady's physician."

Tori stopped rubbing my arm and went still. She stared, waiting for me to do or say something. Even the little girl waited. I couldn't think or speak. There was so much I wanted to say and yet there was nothing I could say. I was numb.

Tori removed her hand and said, "Maybe we should go."

"I'm glad you ran today. It's good to do something like this." He turned and led his family away. His pretty blond wife and little girl number two glanced over her mother's shoulder as they disappeared into the crowd.

Condescending prick. That's what I wanted to say.

"Jen, you're shaking. Do you want to talk?" Tori asked.

I shook my head. She was worried about me. She should be. One minute I was single, then a single mother and now a mother whose child had died of cancer. It was all I could do to stop myself from focusing on the morning before we found out Brady was sick. We had to run out the kitchen door, down the steps and up the lane because Brady had been slow to get out of bed that morning. The little yellow bus was just turning the corner and driving down the street toward us. I recall being so relieved that we wouldn't miss it, because I didn't have time to drive him the school. He trailed behind me struggling to get on his school bag. When I felt his forehead, he was a little warm but well enough to make it to lunch. I'd be able to pick him up then. I thought the doctor would tell me I was worrying about nothing and we'd get pizza on the way home. It had happened before. Everything would be fine.

But not this time. Nothing would ever be fine again.

Tori said, "So Dr. Hodson was Brady's doctor."

I ground my teeth together. "He was the reason Brady died so quickly."

Tori touched my shoulder and a flinched. Her fingers stayed frozen mid-air as she said, "Let's get some coffee. I think you need to sit down for a bit."

The tightness spread across my chest, but I managed to take a deep breath and kept moving. We brushed past people toward the makeshift outdoor café and grabbed two coffees from the food truck. Tori pulled two white, plastic patio chairs together near the edge of the roped off area and we sat.

I held a coffee in one hand and water in the other. Hot and cold. Just like me. Voices swam around us and I let my thoughts drown in them.

"That's better," Tori said smoothing a stray blond hair out of her face. She was always good at filling in awkward lulls in conversation.

I asked, "How do you know him?"

I was a bit surprised to hear my voice. Sometimes I would think about what I wanted to say but after Brady got really sick and I didn't want to hear what the doctors had to say anymore, I couldn't get the words past my lips. Defense mechanism, my mother called it at the time, but what she really wanted to say was I was burying my head in the sand. Not this time.

Tori stared as me for a moment. "We dated once, a million years ago. It was back in University. I don't think we even made it through the second date before it was clear we got along great and would be nothing more than friends. We stayed close for a few years after I graduated, but it got harder to maintain as the years went on. Haven't seen him in…a long time."

I nodded and stared at the stream rising from my coffee.

"Why do you think Jake was responsible for Brady's death?" Jen tried to catch my eye but I wouldn't meet her gaze.

So direct. Most days I didn't mind. In fact, it was because Tori was so direct that I was able to start talking about Brady again. But today I was mad…at her, at Dr. Hodson and at his two perfectly healthy children who would grow up, get married and have long lives.

Tori leaned in. "He was terminal wasn't he?"

"Yes, he was. Dr. Hodson said he was the perfect candidate for a new experimental drug."

"One last hope?"

I nodded. "So I agreed."

Tori stilled, listening hard.

"And I hoped right along with him." The hardness came into my throat, then. This was where I always stopped.

But Tori was listening. Really listening.

"Brady responded badly." I saw him there, so small, so thin, lying on the bed, eyes closed, chest rising and falling so weakly beneath the sheet. Tubes. Tubes in his nose, his arms. The machines, watchful.

"Coma?" Tori's voice was low, barely audible.

"Within hours." I swallowed against the vise grip on my throat. "By the time they realized...it was making him weaker…"

Tori could have interrupted here, told me it was okay, I didn't have to talk about it, didn't have to… but she only took my fingers and looked deep into my eyes. Listening.

"...it was too late. He'd...died a few days later."

Tori nodded her head but didn't say a word.

"Instead of me spending the last few weeks he had left sharing memories and saying goodbye, I spent the last few hours of his life watching him fade away." My eyes pricked and I tried to blink the tears away, but they came anyway.

Tori placed a warm hand on my arm. It must have been the one that had held the coffee.

I pursed my lips and heard the water bottle crinkle in my grip. Breathe. "I miss him so much."

Tori took a deep breath. "Jen, there is nothing I can say to take away your pain but you do know that if they used experimental drugs on Brady, then he was living on borrowed time."

I wiped my eyes with the tips of my fingers. "I just wanted a little more time."

"The longer he lived, the more pain he would have gone through. I know you wouldn't have wanted that for him."

"I wasn't ready to let him go."

"We never are. Jake is an excellent doctor and one of the most compassionate human beings I know. He wouldn't have tried the drug if he didn't believe it might have helped."

I squeezed my eyes tight and listened to the steady beat of my heart. "I know Brady would have passed anyway, but I wanted to say goodbye while he could still hear me."

"He heard you. I'm sure he did, even if he was in a coma." Tori rubbed my back. I used to do that to Brady when he lay in the hospital bed. Her touch was both comforting and devastating.

I wiped my face with my sleeve. "I still feel angry. Dr. Hodson..." the fury rose in my chest again. I'd never said this, not to my mother, not to anyone. "...he cheated me."

"No Jen, Brady would have died...regardless. I'm so sorry."

I lifted my eyes. I opened my mouth then closed it again. The world seemed to tilt on its axis. Brady. I couldn't stop his passing...no one could.

Tori squeezed my arm and I flinched. "I see Jake and his family over there by the energy drinks. I forgot to give him my number, but I'd like to do it before we go. You don't have to come."

"I want to."

"Are you sure you—"

"I am." The corner of my mouth turned up a fraction.

"Okay." I followed behind Tori as she pushed her way through the crowds. Dr. Hodson saw us before the others and stepped forward to meet us.

Tori held out her card and said, "Give me a call sometime Jake, and we'll catch up."

Jake held the card with the tips of his fingers, and stared down at it. "Thanks Tori, I'll do that." He glanced at us and turned to go.

"Dr. Hodson," I said. He froze and turned as though in slow motion. I took a deep breath and swallowed past the lump in my throat. "I just wanted to say…thank you…for everything you did for my son."

He gave a slow nod and said, "Thank you Ms. Artfield, for being the bravest person I know."

I smiled, he turned toward his family and I walked through the crowd with Tori a step behind me. I said over my shoulder, "Looks like the sun's breaking through the clouds. Maybe it'll be a good day to start spring cleaning."

CANADA DAY
by Michael Lalonde

That day she'd turn their son over to him at the train station, Charlie's insides churned at the thought of the encounter. He hadn't seen Billy in a year, couldn't count on one hand the times they'd shared before that. And he would never be left alone with Billy—until now.

Of course, there were the phone calls between Charlie and the ex leading up to this auspicious moment. Calls where Charlie spoke to Billy and enthused over their being in Ottawa for Canada's 150th birthday. 'Sesquicentennial' is how the precocious 12-year-old worded it. Made him proud how the kid had turned out, in spite of his father's shortcomings.

Each phone call was preceded by the 'pep talk' from Christine. Charlie was not to promise Billy anything he could not deliver, and he had to run it by her first. As for the upcoming trip, he had to mind his Ps and Qs with Billy. She insisted that video games and junk food be monitored, and that Billy must respect him as the adult in charge. And in no uncertain terms, Christine forbade his drinking in front of the boy.

When Charlie first saw Christine from a distance, standing on the crowded concourse of the Edmonton station, he was tempted to turn tail and run. His jittery hands longed for a drink. He had wanted something earlier that day to take the edge off, but he didn't dare risk her ensnaring sense of smell.

He'd met his ex-wife in a Fort Mac bar, where her face was made hazy by the tobacco smoke, which hung like sheets in the stale and sour air. Desperate men off rigs (more desperate to return) shouted drink orders to Christine, over the din of hard rock and laugher. And not sure if she'd heard him, Charlie sauntered over from the pool table, to order another beer. She was younger than him—much younger—at least by a decade. And she had many admirers among these sweaty, burly men flush with cash. But never one to back off of a challenge, Charlie used his charm and was triumphant; they bought a house, and inside of three months were married and expecting Billy. Neither ever thought they'd have kids, but at forty, she felt time was running out. Soon after, the economy tanked, and disaster ensued: Jobs lost. Houses repossessed. Marriages broken.

And Charlie found himself today, driving a school bus in the interior of B.C. He lost contact with Christine, now in Edmonton, but through their mutual friend Ronnie, had learned she had a new guy: some big shot engineer named Tim that Ronnie thought was an jerk.

Christine hadn't noticed him yet, and was feverishly checking the time, or something on her cell. He stayed put as she strained to locate him in the crowded railway station. And when there were gaps among the passersby, he caught glimpses of her in a summer dress, slim and sexy as ever. Her long blonde hair used to hang down in her eyes, and she'd launch her bangs upwards, each time she puffed her frustration at him.

But that was another life.

She was a big city girl now. Hair, cut evenly about the shoulders, with a new expensive smile. He'd hardly have recognized her if she hadn't sent that picture last Christmas of herself and Billy, the picture in which the boy came up to her shoulders, skinny as a post in his trunks.

Both were sporting a tan, and holding fancy drinks, at some all-inclusive in the Caribbean. He'd asked her then why Billy hadn't seen the rest of Canada. It was always Disneyland or her boyfriend's timeshare in Mexico. Nothing east of Alberta. Not even Thunder Bay where Billy was born. And that spawned the decision to take his son that summer to Ottawa. "No better place to celebrate Canada Day than in the nation's capital," he'd told her.

Charlie had never been to Ottawa, had no use for politicians of any stripe. A broken promise is all they amounted to. But he had a notion to take Billy east, the way Maman had, when Charlie was his age. It had helped, and though he didn't realize it until years later, it had given him a whole new perspective. Charlie's mother was from Quebec, met his father there when he was travelling through from Alberta. They married, settled in southern Alberta, and Charlie came along one year later.

Christine scanned the station's crowd near her and seemed uncomfortable, as if she'd misplaced something— or someone. Was she looking for him? Perhaps he should have gone to her. But a thought kept him pinned there. Maybe she'd come to say she'd changed her mind, and that she wouldn't let Billy go with him after all.

Then he realized it might not be him she was looking, for Billy was nowhere in sight. Her—searching the immediate surroundings for their son—it went on like this for several minutes. She'd told him frequently that the boy was going through a rough patch—fighting his stepfather. Maybe he'd slipped away, made a break for it.

Charlie could empathize. Around about his ninth birthday, he realized his had not been a perfect life either. It started with a short drive. He and his old man set out for the backwoods in the pickup one night. After crisscrossing bumpy roads that made Charlie's teeth chatter and tossed his body like a rag doll, they pulled over.

"Get your ass out here," his old man said from the rear

of the truck, where he retrieved the jack and heaved it over his shoulder, holding it like a Louisville Slugger.

Charlie stood, facing the slight figure of his dad: A mirror image of him, except taller. "What's that for?" he asked. "Do we have a flat?" But the resemblance faded when his old man's eyes widened and his pockmarked face became strained and contorted.

"Keep quiet."

The old man grabbed him by the scruff of the neck and hauled him up an incline. At the top they scrambled through a thicket of Chokecherry and thistle that scratched at his bare legs until blood trickled down his thighs. Then they crouched at the edge of a clearing. After countless minutes, a chill invaded the clear, night sky rattling Charlie's bones, prodding him to shiver uncontrollably.

"Keep still." The old man said in a low voice as he drove his fingernails into Charlie's scrawny arm, leaving red marks. In the weeks to come, he would tell Maman they were scratches from a stray dog, but he sensed she didn't believe him.

A rustling in the bush across the clearing and a white band appeared, glistening in the moonlight. The skunk shuffled between the shadows of white spruce.

"Wait here," the old man said, and he crept around the clearing until Charlie could see him, crouched low, on the other side.

The first time his old man bludgeoned a skunk, Charlie looked away and cried. The hammer became visible against the stars, the only other witnesses to the brutality. It came down.

Thud. Thud. Thud.

With the sickening monotony of a beating heart. Then the pulse was no more. He quickly wiped away the tears when the approaching silhouette transformed into the solid image of first the old man's blood-spattered pants, then his grinning face. And they said nothing to one another the rest of the way home.

Charlie wondered why he was dragged along. There would be more times, until he was older, and found excuses not to go. When his father drank he took it out on his mother. Charlie began making more excuses, this time for not being home.

When he was ten, he hung out with older boys until the police caught them joyriding in an El Camino. It's when he remembered the old man turning it up a notch, the instant he brought him home from the station. Charlie had been up in his room no more than ten minutes when his parents began to argue. Louder and louder until now they were shouting. Outside his window, their neighbour Mrs. Iverson came into view, gazing their way from her porch. The widow wore a flannel housecoat and had her arms wrapped about herself. She brought her hand up and covered her mouth. What had she seen? That's when the sound of his mother's face being slapped and something smashing against the wall pulled him down the stairs two at a time. He hauled his father off of her. The old man's wide-open mouth of disbelief didn't last, for he raised the back of his hand, and smacked Charlie a good one.

After that, his mother came to him.

"Mon beau," Maman said, pulling him aside. They were out of earshot from his father in the next room, but she cast sidelong glances his way nonetheless, and before speaking once more, pressed a finger to her lips, and shook her head. "You will remember this the rest of your life." And then she retrieved an envelope from her apron, and explained its contents. She'd worked extra shifts at the hotel in Fort Macleod for a year, and bought two economy tickets to travel by train from Calgary to Expo '67 in Montreal. Everyone knew Canada was celebrating its hundredth birthday, with the world making the pilgrimage there. The way she looked at him and then at those tickets, it was as if the two of them were planning an escape. "Just us two, you see?" He nodded knowing what she meant, that his dad wasn't coming, that things would be different when they returned to Calgary.

Charlie remembered the train lurching forward, and his hoping to see his dad on the platform. But the old man had said his goodbyes before setting off to the plant. As if she sensed his angst, Maman squeezed his hand firmly, leaned into him and planted a kiss on his cheek. Charlie wanted to say he missed him, but he did not want to cause more pain for Maman.

The train left the rolling foothills of Alberta behind as it rattled eastward across the expanse of prairie. It slowed down occasionally at small town crossings, where farmers next to trucks gave friendly waves and Charlie waved back. Later he tried to count all of the cows, and then all of the grain elevators along the way. And when he lost interest, he roamed the aisles.

Before long, the darkness of night pressed up against the windows, and the upholstered seats were folded out into beds. The porter came with a special key to let down other beds from the ceiling. And Charlie was thrilled with his upper berth, and the ladder, and the heavy curtains for privacy, and the pillows and sheets that smelled so fresh.

He and Maman had breakfast in the dining car, where the silverware sparkled next to thick linen serviettes. She drank coffee poured for her from a shiny pot, while he sipped chocolate milk from a straw in a glass. And they were waited on like royalty.

When they returned to their car, their beds had magically turned into seats once more, and he saw that Maman was upset. "Your father," she said, looking down at the empty space in her bed, "your father should be here with us." She wanted to cry.

"It's okay, Maman" Charlie said. "It's okay," he kept repeating. He wished he knew what to say, but he was only a boy.

"It's not okay," said Maman. "He should have come to visit my family too." She sniffed and never said another word of it.

36

Toward the middle of the day, the train slowed down. They stopped at the Winnipeg station where Charlie and Maman stepped outside. Charlie couldn't remember it being ever this hot, and there was nothing to see on the platform but people, so he was happy to return to the train. It continued on to Ontario and sped through the night once more. He had never seen an ocean, and was told the sprawling body of water going past them, was not the ocean. A man seated across from them said it was Lake Superior.

Charlie thought he would never see the end of it, and he was only too happy to reach Montreal.

The station was the largest yet, and Charlie worked to fill his lungs with air hot and heavy, not the dry heat he was accustomed to. Maman's sister France would not be there to meet them; she'd sent her husband ahead instead.

A balding man broke from the crowd and approached them. Charlie had not seen him before, but he knew from the description his mother gave him, that this was uncle Jacques. He was short and lean, spry looking, with a tattoo on each forearm: an anchor on one, and a hula dancer on the other. He had blue eyes and sweat beaded down his forehead. He wore a white shirt whose sleeves were rolled up to the elbows, and black pants hoisted by a thick leather belt with a shiny buckle.

"Bonjour, Claire," he said as he kissed Maman. They spoke in French to one another before Jacques turned to Charlie, smiled, and with his big hands lifted him into the air. His uncle had a faint smell of sweat and apples. Jacques spoke French to him, and he was confused.

"On parle en anglais avec le petit," Maman said to Jacques.

Jacques laughed before setting Charlie back down. "Your mother," he said, " she tells me you understand un petit peu—a little bit of French—but don't speak it?" Charlie nodded nervously. Jacques smiled and said, "That's okay son; we all speak a little English here in Quebec."

He helped carry their luggage to his station wagon, and before pulling away, he rolled down a window and lit a cigarette. Soon after, they glided up a ramp, and were catapulted onto Montreal's busy freeways. Everything appeared different to Charlie. Where were all the houses? They passed countless apartments and church spires, and then followed a winding country road until they stopped at a solitary house, so close to the road that Charlie imagined reaching out to touch its front steps. Jacques said the house was built in the horse and buggy days, when the traffic moved much slower. And Charlie wondered if someone could crash into it. The house stood at the top of a slope, and in the distance power lines sagged, liked skipping ropes between towers.

Even with the heat of early evening, many people were gathered around a roaring fire in the backyard. They left their lawn chairs and greeted Maman with hugs and kisses, and Charlie's head spun with all of the introductions. "Charlie," he heard repeated over and over again, the name apparently strange to them, almost comical, as they tried to perfect its pronunciation. He laughed with them. Uncle Jacque explained that his two sons would not be able to meet Charlie that night, that Pierre and Marc were away at summer camp until the next day.

Then a woman appeared from the house, and she was introduced to Charlie as his tante France. She was as tall as Maman with the same hair black as the midnight sky and eyes browner than his own. Over her green dress she wore a flowery apron with its straps tied into a bow on one side of her waist. She smelled like raspberries when she brought him in close for a hug and asked him if he was homesick for his dad. He had not been away from his dad long so he said that he did not miss him yet.

She locked arms with Charlie and Maman and led them to the picnic table with its vast quantity of food: golden fried chicken surrounded by beef ribs, and accompanied by containers of potato salad; stacks of fresh baked buns; and casserole dishes full of pouding chômeur. And there was more than enough beer and wine to go around for the grown-ups.

Later, the last of the taillights faded into the night and a hush settled through the country air. Now there were just the four of them sitting before the stove in the kitchen. Jacques asked Charlie if he noticed his cousin Yvette blushing and staring at him all evening, that he thought Charlie might have a new girlfriend. Charlie glanced at Maman and felt his face go red. He said "No," and they laughed. After telling many jokes and exaggerating the hard work in his beloved apple orchard, Jacques stood and stretched and then went outside to tidy up and ensure the fire outside was extinguished.

Tante France put on a kettle for tea and then let Charlie have a bowl of raspberries from the ones he and his cousins had picked earlier. She smiled at him as she poured cream into his bowl and placed a towel on his lap so he could eat on the nearby rocking chair, and then she sat at the table with Maman.

"You could have come much sooner," Tante France said to her in French. "Was it about the money?"

"No. It's not about the money," Maman responded in French. She glanced Charlie's way and her thoughts were written in her face: How much did he understand? Charlie lowered his eyes to take in a spoonful of raspberries.

"Then what is it? You could have left a year ago, come to Montreal. You'd have found work. There's much of it with the World's Fair. There's a good school for Charlie near our house in Laval. And you could have stayed with us—free."

"I don't need a handout," said Maman a little anxiously. She took a small sip from her cup. "We'll be just fine, thank you."

"But you can't continue living with that man. No, listen. You know how he treats you. How much longer are you going to put up with it? You should have never let him

39

convince you to go live with him out west."

Maman laughed it off. "So you've told me."

Tante France raised her arms and scanned the room about her. "This is your home. This is where you were born. It is where you should have been all along."

Maman became serious all at once. "Listen to me. Do you think it's easy living with someone who drinks? Never knowing if the paycheck is spent before the rent's due? Afraid to ask him what time he'll be home—or if? No. It's not perfect, but I'll manage."

"Manage...manage," Tante France said shifting in her chair. "You have not bought anything new to wear since I saw you last. Look at you. That's the same dress you wore when you left here."

"Pfft, I am not so concerned about material things as some," Maman said, and crossed her arms.

"Think of the boy, then."

"What about the boy?"

"You've told me things." Tante France leaned in. "He deserves better than to be pulled out of school to work for his father. And what is he thinking buying the boy a rifle?"

"—Who told you that?" Maman said, and she followed her sister's eyes. They led back to Charlie. When he noticed them looking his way they turned to one another at once.

Tante France continued in a lower voice. "Jacques said earlier in the evening that the boy boasted of going hunting with his father."

"They go out for drives in the country is all, take fishing rods, but I know of no such rifle."

"Well," Tante France raised her brow, "they are hunting something."

Both now looked at Charlie just as Jacques returned.

"Mon petit," Jacques said, speaking to Charlie in a mixture of French and English. "Le temps d'aller au lit. Little man. Come. It's time for bed. I will show you your room." Charlie kissed Maman and tante France before

Jacques led him away.

It was morning now and Charlie awoke to the clucking of a hen outside his window and the sun shouting its greeting. He heard voices in the upstairs hallway. "I hope I wasn't prying too much last evening," France said above a whisper. "No. I needed to hear that," replied Maman before knocking softly on his door to call him down for breakfast.

In the kitchen Charlie learned that his uncle had left to retrieve Pierre and Marc. He looked forward to meeting his cousins for the first time. Tante France pulled a loaf of bread that had a wonderful yeasty smell from the oven. She set it on a rack to cool and said Charlie could have a slice with butter on it after he picked more raspberries.

Then later in the morning uncle Jacques returned with two tanned boys who stood idly by, each on one side of him. "Here is your cousin Charlie from Alberta." The boys nodded shyly. "This is Pierre," Jacques said as he rested one large hand on the boy to his right, "and this is the youngest, Marc." He ruffled Marc's hair and Marc quickly hand combed it back into form.

Pierre was a year older than Charlie while Marc was a year younger than him, but to Charlie they looked to be the same age. In fact there was not much difference between the three of them in height. However, Pierre had his father's blue eyes and Marc's dark brown ones belonged to Tante France. And Pierre was more fair-haired. But both his cousins had their father's smile: big and infectious.

Their knapsacks reeked from a week's campfires and Tante France insisted they lug them back out onto the porch, and that the three of them stay outside and enjoy the good weather. The three shared with one another what they liked to do in their spare time and Charlie said his father kept him too busy for spare time. And then the other two talked about all of the exciting pavilions they had already seen at Expo and Charlie was at ease with how well they spoke to him in English.

And then they wandered into the barn because his cousins had a surprise for Charlie. The air was thick with the smell of hay and animals. Sunlight strained through to reveal several baskets filled with apples, and to one side they heard the plaintive meow of kittens. The queen had curved her body around them and looked content. And Pierre gently handed one kitten over to Charlie. Its tummy was firm and round and it squirmed in his hands before he set it down once more.

Then they sauntered down the winding rural road to the edge of the village, which had no traffic lights and no sign of life save a brown dog rambling across their path. The sun beat down on them and they ducked under a striped awning in front of the grocery store. From their pocket money they bought ice cream to have in the shade of the towering maple trees in the park. And on the way back to the farm they stopped in at the store once more where they pooled their left over coins to buy the firecrackers.

"Stay away from the house and barn," Tante France said with Maman looking on doubtfully. Charlie knew Maman would never have allowed him to play with firecrackers back home, and his dad, well—he would not have bothered to ask. How lucky his cousins were to have such nice parents, he thought, and he wished he had brothers like Pierre and Marc, wished he was not alone.

The three boys set out well beyond the barn and down the slope into the orchard. And after setting off a few loud bangs one of them got the idea of lodging a firecracker into an apple and then tossing it like a grenade. That led to a search up several ladders leaning against apple trees, but unfortunately Jacque's hired pickers had stripped them bare. So they dashed back up to the barn to fill their pockets with apples from the baskets. And as they exited Charlie eyed one very large apple high up on a shelf and they all agreed that it would make a spectacular explosion.

When all but Charlie's very big apple had been obliterated, and with only two firecrackers remaining, and with much anticipation at having gotten to this point, they stuffed this last apple with both firecrackers. They lit and tossed it high into the heavens where it exploded into breathtaking oblivion. It was a wonder to behold and a satisfying end to their afternoon.

And as they arrived back up at the house, the screen door slapped shut and out exited tante France and uncle Jacques, who remained on the porch as she paraded down the steps, and looking very grave asked, "Pierre, have you seen your father's prize apple, you know, the one he meant to show to the man from the market?" Pierre turned to the other boys who looked at one another and then down at their shoes. Pierre's eyes met hers once more and he nodded.

As Pierre coughed up the truth on the missing apple, Charlie was drawn to the figure of his uncle who appeared more uncomfortable than he was angry, for Jacques folded his arms and then covered his mouth with his great hand. Was that a smile he was hiding? Was he stifling the urge to laugh? Jacques looked at tante France and then at them once more, oddly, as if he was one of the boys. Jacques seemed jealous of their predicament, as if he wished he could have stood there with them as one of the accused. Of course, Charlie realized, uncle Jacques had been one of them—once—had probably faced the scrutiny of grownups in his own time. Jacques was not disturbed by the loss of his prized apple so much as he was jealous in a way that Charlie could not explain. And each time tante France peered back at his uncle, it was as if Jacques had been caught unawares, for he stiffened and nodded as if in agreement with her words.

When the lecturing was all over it was left to Jacques to mete out the punishment. He had the boys lug eight heavy baskets of apples into the station wagon, and the next morning woke them extra early to accompany him to the market in town. Sleepy-eyed, they arrived at the same park where they'd eaten ice cream the day before, and Jacques set up his stand amongst dozens of others beneath the maple trees. He left them to do the selling while he lit up a cigarette and happily roamed among the other vendors.

Charlie and his cousins had a great time talking to the locals and to tourists passing through town, and they took turns pussyfooting about the grounds, taking care not to come to Jacque's attention. When Charlie's turn came up his ears pulled him away to the peculiar sound of a man rapping his hands and knees with wooden spoons while the woman next to him played fiddle and tapped her feet to the music. They supplied Charlie with spoons to play along, and he thought that they were very nice and patient to allow such a beginner to participate.

And that night Charlie asked Maman if he could return to the market and buy a set of spoons for himself. She gave him permission but reminded him that if he'd had to answer to his father for the missing apple, that the ending would not have looked the same. That his father was not so forgiving was something Charlie recognized in his uncle, and he learned that not all fathers were the same.

And now it was the morning three weeks later and the suitcases were in the station wagon. Maman and Charlie said their goodbyes to all but Jacques who was taking them to the train station. Tante France waved to them as the car pulled away. From the rear window Charlie saw Pierre and Marc briefly chase after them then double over with laughter before waving one last time.

Looking at the road ahead Charlie suspected Maman was right about one thing, that he'd remember this trip the rest of his life. They'd travelled across Canada, taken a subway for the first time, toured the great pavilions at expo, and watched fireworks the day Canada turned 100. And when they arrived at the train station his uncle did not lift him into the air the way he had on that first day. Instead he offered his big hand and shook Charlie's saying,

"Remember to come back and visit before we are too old," and he reached into his pocket and gave him an apple.

Billy came into view—standing next to his mother—and Charlie breathed a sigh of relief. She'd allowed him to take Billy after all. He plodded forward and Christine's emerald green eyes caught him coming toward her long before he expected them to.

"No one takes the train anymore," Christine said shortly after greetings. Charlie laughed and became philosophical, making some lame comment about the longest journey being the shortest one to the heart. She didn't get it and as if the moment was awkward enough, he said they had to leave then for the train. As he and Billy marched away he thought of his uncle Jacques who was long gone, and of the many second cousins Billy would meet. And he thought of Maman once more when he said to his son, "You will remember this the rest of your life."

June 3, 2017

Dear Daryl,

I hope you enjoy my story "Of Shadows and Old Homes"

All the very best to you,

Maureen Haseloh

OF SHADOWS AND OLD HOMES
by Maureen Haseloh

My parents, two of my brothers and my two sisters were buried here, hard stones cut with names and dates. My brother William Shea was not buried here. He had died at the battle of Passchendaele in November of 1917. His grave marker was in Belgium, along with markers for thousands of other Canadian soldiers. I carefully laid a long-stemmed sweet-smelling red rose on each of the six tombstones. Then I placed the last rose on the ground in front of my parents' grave, in memory of William. I 'the baby of the family' had outlived them all.

I glanced at my granddaughter, squatting nearby, her dark waist-length hair sweeping the grass. She moved forward to study each tombstone. Balancing a pad of paper on her knee, she wrote, pen soaring across the page. The wind tossed her hair and she bunched it up impatiently and threw it behind her.

After Marion had finished looking at the graves, she stood up and put the pen and paper into her large cloth purse.

"Well Marion, I've placed the flowers. We've paid our respects. Were you copying down all the dates?" I asked, secretly hoping she had. One of us should keep track of these things. Birthdays and death days, the numbers blurred in my mind.

"Yes. I copied the names and dates of all of them. The

only ones that were hard to read were the tombstones of your parents. Those dates were eroded. But I managed: James Shea, born 1870 and died 1910. He was only 40 when he died! Margaret Shea, born 1869 and died 1930. I guess women did live longer than men in the old days," she said. She gave me her arm as we walked away from the family plot.

"Women do tend to be the survivors," I agreed. Even though most of the birthdays and death days did elude me, I did remember two important dates. "If you are keeping track, your great-uncle William Shea was born January 28, 1893. He died in World War I and the date on the death register was November 10, 1917." I did remember his birthday and his death day because his death had been such a tragedy for our family.

Marion stopped and said, "Wait a minute Grandma. I will write that down." She retrieved her pad of paper and I repeated the dates for her. She bent over and put the pad of paper on her knee. After she wrote down my brother's information, we continued to walk through the Brandon graveyard that was crowded with white lambs and crosses. The chilly Manitoba wind breathed through the trees, rustling the thick green leaves. The clouds were grey pillows, waiting to burst at the seams. I could smell approaching rain.

"I'm so glad we came Grandma. I'm always inspired by graveyards," Marion said and we stepped into the waiting taxi parked at the edge of the cemetery. Once we were seated inside, she closed the back door. "So many poetic inscriptions and untold stories. Don't you agree?"

I didn't answer for a moment, feeling the pain of loss more than inspiration from the epitaphs. I opted for tact and said, "Well Marion, you have a unique way of seeing things. I'll say that."

Brandon is small, so it was a short journey home. I paid the driver and clutched Marion's arm for support as I emerged from the taxi.

I held her left arm and looked at the home that my mother had built. It always filled me with pride; three storeys high, the tallest house for miles. Apple green for decades until I had it painted peach with white trim. The veranda was pink, partly covered with green carpet. An ivory-colored railing encircled the veranda that had serviced four generations.

Marion unlatched the wire mesh gate with her free hand. She held it open and we proceeded up the broken sidewalk. We climbed the stairs, one step at a time. I used the black railing for support and moved slowly, feeling some pain in my back. Osteoporosis was the price of a long life, I thought. "Sorry Marion. I need to sit down as soon as we get inside."

"Grandma! Don't apologize. You are doing great for your age," Marion said as she unlocked the heavy oak door and pushed it open. She waited for me to enter first. "When we heard that you fell and broke your arm this past winter, Mom hoped you would move out West so we could take care of you. Your arm is healing nicely."

Surprisingly, my arm did not hurt as much as my back. The idea of moving out West was never far from my mind. I did need to make a decision about whether I could keep living here. I missed having family around. It was plain good fortune that Marion had the time to come here and be with me now. "You're quite a girl Marion. Quite a girl. Let's have the three t's," I said as I sank down onto the hall chair to remove my rubber boots.

Marion went to put the kettle on and I followed her down the hall. I sat on the bench by the kitchen table, waiting for tea and toast and talk.

I wondered what Marion must think of my kitchen. The kitchen was for family only. (Visitors took their tea in the parlor.) The walls were salmon pink and the paint was chipping, peeling off the walls. The porcelain sink was stained from countless teabags. The house had long been more of a hospital than a place of entertainment. My family had lived and died here and I had been their nurse.

The only light was a bulb hanging from the middle of the ceiling. To turn it on and off, you pulled the low-hanging chain until it snapped. We'd been grateful for electricity, never mind the accoutrements. We had been fortunate because we always had what we needed. I thought of our telephone.

"Marion, did you know that we were the first family on this block to have a telephone? We needed a telephone when Mother was sick. I remember calling the doctor and he would come to the house. In those days doctors made house calls."

"Interesting. What was your phone number?" Marion asked.

"Our phone number was 3 2 7 4," I said, happy that I could still remember the old phone number. It had since changed to a seven-digit number. "The neighbors used to come to our house and borrow our telephone."

"It is hard to believe that your phone number was only four digits!" Marion said.

The tea kettle whistled loudly, steam spilling into the air. Marion lifted it off the burner. It was too heavy for me to pick up. She poured the boiling water into the white Spode teapot, where I had snuck an extra teabag when she wasn't looking.

She sat across from me, bunching her hair and throwing it so that it fell down her back. "You know, I don't know anyone in the world that I'd rather have tea with than you Grandma," Marion said and smiled. "This is such a treat. To have you all to myself for four weeks. No sisters or brothers or parents! Just you and me. Here in peaceful Brandon, Manitoba."

"It worked out very well," I agreed, thinking about how lonely it had been in this house since my brother Clifford died. The last one. I was happy to have Marion's company. "What will we do this summer? I don't know any young people."

"I've thought about this trip a lot, and what I'd really like to do this summer is decide what I want to do with my life. What courses to take in the fall. I'm eighteen you know. In September I'll be in university."

"It seems like just yesterday you were in kindergarten. I remember visiting when you first learned how to read. You and your books. Inseparable. And now you're finished high school."

"Amen!" Marion said fervently. "Tomorrow I am going to the library. I can't wait to explore the Brandon Public Library. I visit our neighborhood Calgary library every week." She bit into her toast.

I preferred dunking my toast in my tea. Nice and soggy, easy to chew with these awful dentures.

That night, we slept well and woke up to a sunny day. We enjoyed a simple breakfast of cereal together in the kitchen.

A few hours after Marion left for the library, I went upstairs.

I went to each room and collected dirty laundry. I removed used towels from the bathroom and then collected bedding and clothing items from the bedrooms. I put it all into the laundry chute on the second floor where it sailed down to the basement clothes basket. This three-storey house had certainly needed a laundry chute when Mother had the three boys on the third floor and her, my sisters and me on the second floor. I could remember the clothes getting stuck and one of the boys using a broom handle to dislodge the tight bundle of clothes until it sailed to the basement.

I had hired a laundry service a few years ago when our wringer washing machine had quit working. I had arranged to have them pick up the dirty laundry in the basement. I left the back door unlocked and the laundry delivery people came and went once a week. It was one of the luxuries that enabled me to keep my independence.

I had a rest on my bed and fell into a sound sleep. I had

51

just come downstairs when Marion returned from the library, her arms loaded high with books.

"How did you ever manage Marion?" I asked, watching her fumble and spill the tall load of books onto the hardwood floor at our feet.

"Where there's a will as strong as mine, there's a way. I took a taxi!"

We laughed. She gathered her hair and threw it behind her, and then she carefully piled the books against her chest, and slowly rose and walked under the weight of the books to the dining room. She piled the books on the dining room table.

I glanced in the hall mirror and saw a dark long curly perm edged with grey. It needed coloring-I'd never go grey. Bright blue eyes, the one thing that hadn't been slapped with Time's merciless hand. My back was permanently stooped. Dusty green polyester pants were held up by a diaper safety pin. I wore a white blouse. I opened my lipstick and touched up my lips while I was standing there. The rouge on my cheeks matched my bright red lipstick.

Marion met me in the hall. "You don't mind if I start reading do you Grandma? We'll have tea later."

"Not at all. Not at all." I did mind a little.

She settled on the plum-colored velvet sofa in the parlor. The window next to her looked onto the veranda. A fireplace of orange plastic logs with light bulbs inside gave the illusion of warmth on cold winter days. But it was summer now, another summer.

I left Marion to her books and went into the dining room to write my letters. With a press of a switch, the low-hanging chandelier lit up the room. Unlike the kitchen, Mother had invested in expensive lighting for the dining room. I sat on one of the mahogany chairs and wrote letters to my daughters and grandchildren. I wrote about Marion's safe arrival, our visit to the cemetery and the impending rain.

When I'd finished, we sat down to Marion's supper of eggs on toast and a cup of tea.

"Now tell me, how was the library?" I asked.

"It was cozy. I did find a few books. And the bus ride there was scenic. Long but scenic. We passed wheat and corn fields. Does the bus always go out to the country before going downtown?" Marion asked in awe.

"Yes. If you catch it in front of this house. We used to own a farm out there. Close to the town of Alexander where I was born. You know what Cliff said after I was born? He said, 'Take her back! Look at those curls! Take her back!' As if my curls were a crime."

"You miss Uncle Clifford don't you?"

"Yes. Yes I do. We had our ups and downs mind you. But we had each other. We used to watch the "Lawrence Welk" show every Saturday night. I'd make a pot of tea and we'd eat a fresh marble cake with thick chocolate icing. I'd say, 'Come on old boy. Your show is on.' And he'd amble down the stairs. How I enjoyed watching that show with Cliff! I liked the accordion player. He looked just like your grandpa. Andrew was a good-looking fellow," I said, and turned my wedding ring around and around. Even though he had died 20 years ago, I still missed him so much. How I'd love to talk to him now. He always had such good advice.

As the days passed, I was grateful that Marion could entertain herself. She enjoyed reading and writing and did not need people her own age to entertain her. We ate, slept and enjoyed our pastimes. It was a simple time, overshadowed only by our need to make major life decisions.

One afternoon, I sat in the dining room armchair with my needles and wool. I was knitting a mauve scarf for Marion's mother. Luckily, my fractured arm had healed enough for me to take up knitting again. I liked knitting. It made me feel productive and it gave me time to think. In two more weeks Marion would be leaving. I felt like going with her. She was my tea-maker, cook and friend. My granddaughter. Her mother had repeatedly told me that I was welcome to live with them. But move out West? I didn't want to be a burden on my daughter, but simple tasks had escalated into insurmountable obstacles. In the months after Cliff's death and before Marion's arrival, I had given up tea altogether. I just did not have the strength to lift the kettle. For a few days, all I had eaten was toast. But this was my home! My roots were here. Could I adjust to Calgary? Did I have a choice? I was knitting madly away in a sea of thought when Marion entered the dining room with the teapot.

"Bless your heart. A cup of tea," I said, glad of the temporary respite from my own musings. She placed the white teapot on the table.

"Grandma, let's talk. I'm getting really frustrated."

You're not the only one, I thought to myself. When she returned to the kitchen to get tea cups, I removed a tea bag from my pocket and surreptitiously added it to the hot water in the teapot.

"What's the matter?" I asked when she returned a moment later balancing tea cups, saucers and a plate of crackers and sliced cheese. She looked peaked. No wonder. She rarely went outside. I left my knitting on the overstuffed chair and joined her at the dining room table.

She poured our tea. While we ate cheese and crackers and drank our tea, she said between bites, "I've read books about several careers that interest me. I've considered several careers. Veterinarian, pharmacist, teacher, psychologist, policewoman, hotel manager and chef. I am not enthused about any of these options."

I had to hide a smile when she said chef. She was one of the least ambitious cooks I'd ever seen.

I leaned forward and held her hand. "Marion. Don't be discouraged. Figuring out what you don't want to do is an essential step in figuring out what you do want to do. The process of elimination," I said and patted her hand for a moment.

"I will think about that. Thanks Grandma. You know, those career books were a big help in showing me what I'm not. I guess it's time to abandon those books. It's time to get personal and read through all my old diaries and journals. Maybe then I'll find myself. Do you remember my small trunk that you said looked so heavy? Well it is full of my old diaries, notes and all kinds of memorabilia. I am going to organize it all into a chronological package and see if I can find myself there. Meanwhile, I'd better set the table. Would you rather have hot dogs or eggs on toast?" she asked, getting up from her chair.

"Hot dogs would be lovely dear," I said.

While Marion made supper, I went back to my knitting. The scarf was getting quite long. I mentally weighed the pros and cons about my own decision. I didn't want to worry about this rambling old house anymore and yet selling my family home seemed disloyal. I didn't enjoy eating alone. I did not want to be a problem for my daughter. I missed her. I missed having family around. I didn't want to leave Brandon and give up my independence. I sighed.

We sat down to supper in the kitchen a few minutes later. We passed the knife back and forth between us, as we used it to spread mustard and relish on the hot dog buns. Marion hated doing dishes so we used as few as possible.

Marion asked, "Grandma, can you tell me a story about this house? I was just thinking that there must have been some interesting things that happened here."

I said, "I do have a story. In the 1930's, during the Great Depression, there was a lot of unemployment. Unemployed men would ride the rails searching for work. Since the train stops close to this house, there was frequent freight-hopping. Some of these men would get off the train and come to our house. We always had enough food and we would feed these hobos. I discovered that our house was marked with a circled X. That symbol meant that we were a good place for them to get a handout. I remember my sister Gertrude giving a hobo stewed tomatoes on bread. He was just ravenous! He sat on the back steps and ate with more enjoyment than anyone I have ever seen."

"I am glad you fed the hobos. It makes me happy that my relatives were so kind," Marion said with a smile.

The circled X. I had not thought of that in a long time. It was another part of this home's precious history.

After supper, Marion was buried in papers, writing madly. I sat at one end of the long dining room table alternating between knitting and writing letters, while she sat at the other end reading and taking notes.

Lengthy shadows and rays of sunlight splayed across the cluttered table, a never-ending intercourse of darkness and light.

As the summer passed, I kept postponing my inevitable decision about where to live out the rest of my days.

The house was quiet except when she turned the big radio on and we listened to classical music. I preferred bands like 'The Ink Spots', but I did enjoy the classics.

One evening, a few days before her departure, Marion entered the kitchen sighing loudly.

"Is everything okay? How are your diaries coming?" I asked.

"Well it's a long process but I'm almost caught up to February of this year. I've written about absolutely everything that I can remember. And I haven't stumbled on the answer."

"If you want to be happy, you'll have to do what you love. I loved caring for the sick so I became a nurse. Your great-aunt Gertrude loved teaching so she became a teacher. Bless her soul." I wished I could give Marion a magic answer.

"Thanks Grandma. You've been a big help. I'm going for a walk to clear my head. I haven't been outside for days!"

After Marion left, I glanced in the hall mirror. I focused on my still bright eyes and decided that being old wasn't so bad. Not when you could still help someone else. Now it was time to help myself.

I went into the dining room and sat down with paper and a pen. I wrote a list of pros and cons about moving to Calgary. Even a veteran pros-and-cons-list-maker like me had a moment of self-doubt as the pros outweighed the cons. I looked around the dining room which had once echoed with the laughter and voices of my brothers and sisters. The smell of fruitcake baking when Minnie did her Christmas baking. Her fruitcake was always eaten up before Christmas even arrived! Easter vigil. Birthday celebrations. The joy we felt when my sister Gertrude arrived home for the summer after her teaching year ended. Cliff forgetting to take his hat off in the house. Having Tom come home for holidays. And a long time ago, Mother telling Cliff to quit pretending that I was adopted. At the bottom of my list I wrote in big letters: PEOPLE ARE MORE IMPORTANT THAN PLACES.

I waited for Marion to return. When she did, her dark long hair was drenched with rain dripping off it.

"Grandma do you know what I discovered on my walk?" she asked each hand alternately on the door handle as the other hand removed a boot. She left her boots on the veranda to dry, before slamming the big oak door shut in her excitement.

"What?" I asked as I helped her get the black raincoat off and hung it on a coat hook.

We adjourned to the plum-colored sofa in the parlor.

"I can't let things pass without recording and sharing them. Or they'll disappear into the darkness. You know how you pay your respects to the dead by visiting their graves? Well I am here to pay respects to both the living and the dead by writing their stories. I want to get an English degree and become a writer."

"You want to be a writer! Good choice. 'Marion-the author!'" I said, punctuating the air with my index finger.

"Yes! A writer! I thought about what I really enjoy. I've enjoyed this summer with you more than anything I've ever done. And what have I been doing? Reading, researching and writing." Her heart's vision shone in her Irish eyes.

"Marion, I am so pleased that you have chosen a career path. I think you have made an excellent choice. You always loved books. Now, I have some news for you. You are the first one I am going to tell. I have decided to move out West. Taking care of this big house and living alone is not working for me. I miss family and it is time to move on." Saying the words out loud was such a relief to me.

"Grandma, I am SO happy to hear that. Let's call Mom right now and tell her the good news," Marion said.

When we called my daughter and I told her my decision, she said, "Mom, I am very relieved. I will get your room ready. I am so glad you are moving out west! We have all been worried about you. We want you to come as soon as possible."

I said, "Thank you dear. I will be on the same train as Marion. I look forward to seeing you all!"

After we signed off, I said to Marion, "I am coming home with you!"

I could not stay in this wonderful old house anymore. I once heard that you have to love something before you can leave it. And I loved this old home. But I could not stay here just for the memories. It was time to leave. After hearing my daughter's voice, I realized how important my family was.

I was going home.

And home was family.

THE YELPING DOG CAMPGROUND
by Allison Gorner

I don't know how to tell my story. It sounds so outrageous, I must be making it up. But it's true. All the rumours I heard before this happened, about the monstrous creature roaming the woods, hiding in caves, feasting on its prey, they're all true. I sure wish they weren't. It's not like in Scooby-Doo where there's always a rational explanation for the ghosts and monsters. But at the end it's just the embittered gardener with a rubber mask. This was real. No gardener. No rubber masks. Just plain old freaky.

But I'm getting ahead of myself. You probably don't even know what I'm talking about. I'll start at the beginning.

My name is Hannah and I am twelve. I'm a normal girl in a normal town with a normal life. You could say it's boring. I even look normal. Ordinary brown hair. Boring hazel eyes. I'm not short, not tall. I'm completely average. If you were to see me on the street, you wouldn't notice me, and you definitely wouldn't remember me. I'm a regular girl.

I have a younger (and annoying) brother Nick who's ten, and he's the one that got me into this mess. But more about that later.

I guess my story starts with our summer vacation. My parents decided that it would be more "fun" if we left the comfort of our home, or even a hotel, and go camping all summer.

"Let's have a real vacation," my dad said. "None of this overcrowded, overpriced Disneyland stuff."

"We're going to Disneyland! Woo-hoo!!" shouted Nick.

"No, no," Dad blurted.

"Of course not," I said. "Disneyland wouldn't fit into our normal, boring lives. That's too exciting for our family."

Dad continued like he hadn't heard me, "We're going camping!"

I stared at him, unblinking.

"Real camping. We'll use firewood and sleeping bags and make all our food on the open flame! It will be a blast!"

Nick groaned loudly.

"Just you wait," said Dad. "We'll have hotdogs and marshmallows and lots of good old fashioned fun!"

So a few days later Nick and I crammed into the back seat of our car with all the camping gear and no room to breathe. All in pursuit of "good old fashioned fun." Yippee.

Nick soon fell asleep and snored, right in my ear. I wiggled as far away from him as I could and squashed myself against the window watching the changing landscape whizz by. Then it rained.

"Perfect," I muttered.

Get ready for the worst vacation ever. Little did I know how true that would be.

* * *

Our first two weeks were boring and uneventful unless you counted the rain. It rained for almost 10 days straight. Nick and I settled in our tent staying relatively dry playing cards or reading while Mom dutifully followed Dad on "fun outdoor activities" that I refused to take part in. I would not risk my health for the sake of a nature hike in the cold rain and deep mud.

Finally Dad gave into our pleadings and decided to find another campground with actual sunshine.

We drove for hours looking for a specific campground Dad remembered reading about in his new book 'The Top 100 Campgrounds in Western Canada.' Only he couldn't remember which one it was.

"I know the name is in there somewhere," Dad said to Mom. "Just keep reading. I'm sure I'll remember when I hear it."

"There are over a hundred! It'll take me forever to read these out to you."

"Just start at the beginning."

"Why don't you pull over and then you can look at the book yourself. That will probably be quicker."

"I don't want to lose any time pulling over when we could be driving. What if the campground's only ten minutes away, I see the sign, remember, and then we're there? If we pull over, we'll waste at least half an hour."

"What if you see the sign and don't remember," said Nick. "Then we would have to turn around when Mom finally finds the campground in the book."

"Impossible," Dad grunted. "Wouldn't happen."

"But if it did," I said, "I wouldn't mind. At least we'd be dry and warm in the car all day."

Dad just grunted again while Mom read the list of campgrounds from the index. Sometimes Dad would ask Mom to describe a name he thought he recognized. Not until Mom got to the "Y's" did Dad remember.

"The Yearly Retreat," Mom said sounding bored.

"Nope."

"The Yelping Dog Campground."

"That's the one!"

Nick and I snickered.

"The Yelping Dog!?" Mom asked. "That's the name you got so excited about? What's so special about that?"

"Yeah, sounds like a dive," Nick said.

"Now c'mon," said Dad. "It sounds exciting! I remember now. There's a lake, canoes, hikes in the woods, and even a historical graveyard. Now that sounds cool."

"Nothing with the word historical sounds cool," said Nick.

"There are cabins!" said Dad trying to convince us.

That caught my attention. If we stayed in a cabin, the rest of the vacation wouldn't be half so miserable.

"Can we really stay in a cabin, Dad? Please?" I asked.

"Well, there are real campsites too. We have tents."

"Cabin! Cabin! Cabin!" Nick chanted.

"Cabin! Cabin!" I joined in.

"Oh all right, all right. We can stay in a cabin."

"Yeah!!"

By the time we finally got to The Yelping Dog Campground, it was already dark. Nick slept, drooling all over the seat. Dad pulled up to the registration booth.

"G'evenin'" said a man at the window. He looked ancient and withered. Only a few teeth were left in his crooked grin and he had two tufts of grey hair, one above each ear. It looked like he had been sitting in that booth his whole life. I almost expected to see cobwebs connecting him to the wall. I'm sure if I were any closer, I would smell him too.

"Good evening," said Dad. "Do you have any cabins left tonight?"

"Sure do. Cabin thirteen."

"We'll take it."

The man handed Dad some papers and I swear I heard his bones creak as he reached towards the window.

"By the way," said Dad as he passed back the paperwork and some cash, "Why is the campground called the Yelping Dog?"

"Well, I reckon it's on account of the dog that yelps."

"All right, thanks," said Dad, confused.

The cabin seemed warm and cozy, at least the bed was.

I remember little about my surroundings that first night because I was so tired and so glad to be on a mattress, and not on the damp, cold, rocky ground.

I was just drifting into sleep when a horrible sound jolted me awake. An unearthly howl pierced the night. It wailed and howled and chilled me to the bone. Was that the yelping dog? It sure didn't sound like a dog and it definitely wasn't yelping. I'd never heard anything like it. It was irritating like nails being scraped on a chalkboard, but frightening like the wail of a banshee. I covered my ears and ducked under my blankets, but it wasn't enough to drown out the howl. Abruptly the sound stopped, and the night was quiet and still.

* * *

Warm sunshine shone on my face as I woke the next morning. The sun! I had almost forgotten that it even existed. I jumped out of bed and dressed. Maybe we could actually do something fun today, like swimming or canoeing.

When I got to the little kitchen, Dad was already making breakfast. It smelled good.

"What's for breakfast, Dad?" I asked.

"Banana pancakes for my Hannah-Banana," he said with a stupid grin.

I hate it when he calls me Hannah-Banana. I'm not three years old anymore. I mostly ignored it this time because I love banana pancakes. But I rolled my eyes to show my disapproval. He pretended not to notice, but I know he did. It worked because he didn't call me Hannah-Banana again.

As I was eating my seventh delicious pancake, Nick came out of his room. Food always wakes him up. His messy short brown hair stuck straight up in the front and matted down in the back. He looked ridiculous. He sat down, rubbed his eyes and plopped his head down on the table.

"Hmpff!" I laughed. Little pieces of bananas and pancakes soaked in syrup flew unintentionally out of my mouth and landed within inches of Nick's protruding hair. Good thing he didn't notice.

"What?" he mumbled grumpily. He's always grumpy in the morning.

I swallowed my pancakes. "Your hair! You look so dumb!"

"You always look dumb," he replied.

"Kids," said Mom sternly as she came into the room, "No fighting before I've had my breakfast."

"Now when she's done her breakfast, feel free to fight as much as you like," said Dad winking at us. Nick and I chuckled.

"That's not what I meant, and you know it." Mom glared at Dad.

Dad just turned, shrugged and flipped more pancakes.

After devouring five more pancakes I headed outside with a book, my beach towel and wearing my swimsuit under my clothes. I was looking forward to some quiet when I heard a scuffling noise behind me. I turned around to see Nick's head peering around the propped open front door. He glanced wildly around. Apparently the coast was clear because he came out.

"Where are you going?" he said.

"To the beach. Without you."

"You can't stop me," he said coming to stand next to me. Nervous, he swung his head back and forth, peering into the trees.

"What are you doing? Why are you acting so weird?"

"Weird? I'm not acting weird." Nick took a step closer and grabbed onto my towel.

"Yes you are," I said as I yanked my towel out of his hand. "Go find someone else to bug."

Leaving Nick on the porch, I followed the path away from the cabin in the direction I thought the lake was in.

Lining the path were the most sorry trees I have ever seen. Bare and leafless the dried up old branches barely clung to the blackened trunks. An entire forest of brittle, dead trees. Many tilted to the side as if they would fall over any moment. There were a few that had. No grass grew on the ground, no foliage of any kind. I didn't see any animals or hear any birds. Everything was dead. Super creepy.

I hurried along and soon reached a fork in the path with an old signpost. The painted letters were flaking and peeling away. It took a moment to decipher the signs. Lake pointed left, Gatehouse right. Cabin 13 pointed to the path behind me.

I turned to the left hurrying away from the dead trees and toward the openness of the lake when I heard a shuffling sound behind me. I whipped around. Nothing there. It was just a squirrel, I thought. Then I remembered the deadness of the woods. What kind of animal could possibly live in there? I walked a little faster.

Crack! The sound echoed through the trees. I turned again. Still nothing. Was it a bear? Or a cougar? I ran. A cacophony of sounds followed behind me; rustling, cracking, shuffling, breathing. Something was chasing me!

I ran harder, not daring to look behind.

"Hannah!" I heard. "Stop!"

Nick? I stopped running and turned. He was running to catch up with me.

"Nick!" I shouted angrily between heavy breaths. "What are you doing? Why are you sneaking up on me?"

"I didn't... I wasn't..." he got out as he reached me.

"Go back to the cabin."

"Wait," said Nick a little desperately. "Mom and Dad left to get ice. I don't want to be alone."

"Aww... is little Nicky scared?" I said forgetting all about my earlier fright.

"No!"

"Then go back."

"It's j-j-just..." Nick stammered. "Didn't you hear it?"

"Hear what, Nick?" I was getting impatient.

"Last night… that sound."

Suddenly it came rushing back. The unearthly banshee yell in the dead of night. The creepy tingling sensation on the back of my neck. How I wanted to disappear under my blankets and never come out.

"You did hear it!" Nick said seeing my face.

"So what if I did?" I said, my mind returning to the present.

"Aren't you scared?"

"No," I lied.

"Well, I am. And I'm not staying alone in that cabin for nothing!"

"Fine then come along. See what I care."

I turned and continued along the path to the lake. Nick followed close behind me. Soon the trail led to a break in the trees and we could see the lake.

To say the lake was disappointing would be a massive understatement. It wasn't even a lake. More like a large pond. Thick green pond scum covered the entire surface of the water. Sickly green tendrils crept up the rocky shore. It reeked of manure. It made me think of Creature From The Black Lagoon, an old horror movie my dad showed me once when my mom wasn't home. The creature and the scum were exactly the same colour. I put my towel and book down on the least scummy rock. I would not be swimming.

"What is that smell?!" Nick exclaimed. "Was that you? I think I'm gonna hurl." He made fake retching noises as I glared at him.

"Quiet now," said a raspy voice. I startled and turned.

The old man from the registration booth was standing waist deep in the putrid muck. He had on rubber overalls that reached up to his chest and no shirt. The skin on his arms draped off the bone, wagging as he moved. He held a large fishing net, his hands enclosed in thick industrial rubber gloves. He didn't look at us but scrutinised the water.

"What are you doing?" Nick asked.

Like a shot the man plunged the net into the pond and brought it out again. A silver fish now wriggled helplessly inside.

"You're fast for an old guy. And skinny." Nick didn't have a filter. I agreed, but at least I didn't say it out loud.

"Yup," the man replied.

His boots squelched as he tromped out of the muck. Scum clung to his overalls making his bottom half resemble slimy fur. I smiled to myself. Maybe he was the creature from the Black Lagoon. Or the creature from the scummy pond.

He placed his net on the ground next to a pile of about twenty fish I hadn't noticed before. Gripping his catch by the tail, he smashed its head on the rocks. The fish stopped wriggling. I grimaced. Pulling a knife from somewhere under his overalls, he filleted the freshly caught fish.

Fascinated, Nick move closer. His eyes bulged as the knife seared through flesh. "What's your name?"

"Earl. What's yours?"

"Nick, and this is my sister Hannah. How did you catch it? I mean, could you even see it through all that green stuff?"

"Nope. Couldn't see it. Heard it."

"That's ridiculous." I said. "You can't hear fish." I moved closer, but not too close. I didn't want to see fish guts.

Earl looked up at me. "All animals make noise. Fish too. You just gotta know what to listen for. Like that noise…" His gazed shifted from my face to the woods behind me. He slowly stood holding the knife out in front of him. "Is a grizzly bear."

Snuffling and rustling sounds came from behind me. I grabbed Nick's arm and pulled him behind the old man and away from the bear.

Unmoving, Earl stared towards the trailhead, knife out, ready to spring. A large hairy shape prowled in the bushes, sheltered by the trees.

"See that other trail?" Earl whispered gesturing his head further down the tree line toward a small partially hidden path. "When I yell, you run. Go back to your cabin."

The rustling grew louder. Nick whimpered and squeezed my hand hard. I squeezed back reassuringly, trying to hide how frightened I was. The grizzly moved to the edge of the trees. It lifted on his powerful hind legs raising eight feet into the air. With dark, matted fur and half in shadow I couldn't make out the bear's features. But something seemed horribly wrong. Before my brain could register what that was, Earl yelled and charged the beast. Nick and I bolted down the small trail. We didn't look back. I ran hard, pulling Nick along, my breath rough and fast.

A tall, crumbling, brick wall loomed ahead with a massive wrought iron gate. We ran to it and I grabbed the latch. The metal groaned as I swung it open and pushed my brother inside. Together we heaved the gate shut and slid the bolt into place. I sunk down in the dirt exhausted and terrified. Nick collapsed down beside me.

"Did you see that?" he said. Sweat dripped down his face. He looked as horrified as I felt.

"Kind of. Something's not right," I said shaking my head.

"That was not a grizzly. Hannah, that was a sasquatch!"

"Sasquatches aren't real." A shriek pierced the air. A screech, growl and harsh cry all in one. The banshee yell from the night before. The hair on my arms stood up on end. I shivered.

"See?" he said, his voice shaking. "It's the war cry of the sasquatch!"

I couldn't dispute him. What animal made that yell? Was there a giant furry ape-man living in the woods?

"Well, let's wait here for a while," I said, wary. "Where are we anyway?"

The old brick wall enclosed an area the size of a basketball gym. At least twelve feet high, the wall cast large, dark shadows. Gravestones in crooked rows lined the ground. A small mausoleum stood in the centre, the door hanging from its hinges. The old graveyard lay still, unkempt and decaying. No one had been here for years.

"This must be the historical graveyard dad told us about," I said.

"Ghosts are better than sasquatches, right? At least they can't bite you." His little chuckle died away quickly.

"I think we're safe in here from the... whatever that was."

"Sas-quatch," he said elongating the syllables. "Just say it." Another monster yell rung out. Far in the distance this time. We quickly scrambled across the dirt and ducked behind the nearest gravestone.

"Sasquatch! Sasquatch! I said it, you happy?"

"Do you think Earl is ok?" Nick whispered.

For a long time we sat in uncomfortable silence examining the carved letters in the headstone. EDGAR EARL 1841 - 1923. My finger traced the "G." They can't be real, I thought.

The gates rattled and shook. Nick screamed in fright. I pressed my face against the name, hiding as much of myself behind the slab as possible.

"Nick? Are you in there? Hannah?"

"Dad!" I called relieved. "We're here." I came out of my hiding place and unlocked the gate.

"I've been looking for you. You missed lunch," Dad scolded. "I found your things by the lake and you weren't there. I was worried."

"Dad! Dad! You'll never guess what we saw," Nick ran at dad and grabbed his shirtsleeve. "A sasquatch! We ran, but it attacked Earl. We need to see if he's ok."

"You mean Mr. Earl? The caretaker? He's fine," Dad said confused. "No, he came by the cabin to bring extra firewood. He acted surprised you guys weren't there and wanted to apologize for telling tall tales about grizzlies. He thinks he scared you."

"It's not a grizzly, it's a sasquatch," Nick insisted.

"Sasquatch stories, eh? Well no wonder you got scared." Dad chuckled.

"But," I said.

"No more buts. Let's get back. Mom made sloppy Joes."

* * *

Nick ate in silence. He normally jabbers on about hockey or Pokémon or other stupid things. Tonight he was mad. Mom and Dad didn't believe him. I didn't back him up. He scowled at me over the sloppy Joes. My saying anything would only make it worse. He stomped off to bed in a huff after losing at Uno. I played a few more games with mom and dad then headed to our bedroom.

"Nick," I whispered. I felt bad for abandoning him. He didn't answer. "C'mon. I'm sorry."

I tried to shake his shoulder but squished pillows instead. Pulling back the blanket I found more pillows. He wasn't there.

"Mom! Dad! Nick's gone!"

My parents rushed into the room. Mom stared at the pillows and stifled a sob. Dad said, "I'll get Mr. Earl," and rushed out of the room.

When Dad and Earl returned mom was frantic. Seeing Earl's rifle sent her into hysterics.

"Sir, stay with your wife. Hannah, grab a flashlight and come with me," Earl said.

I grabbed my flashlight as dad spluttered in protest and followed Earl outside.

"Follow me and stay close," he said.

I flicked on my flashlight and tried to keep up with Earl's long strides. We followed the path through the dead forest to the pond, the blackened trees silent and eerie. I stilled an unsettling shiver and said, "You said your name is Earl. Why did my dad call you Mr. Earl?" I actually wanted to ask him why he lied to my parents. But he would say I'm being rude and send me back to the cabin.

"My surname is Earl. Most people just call me that."

"Who's Edgar Earl? I saw his name on a gravestone."

"That's my grand pappy. Brave man." He stopped, and I almost bumped into him. "Turn off your light now."

"But I can't see without it," I complained.

"I can. Follow me."

I followed in darkness, my eyes struggling to adjust. We broke through the tree line to the pond. It still reeked but at least the moon was visible here. He crouched down by the water's edge scanning the rocks, the scum, and I don't know what. Apparently it satisfied him. "Hmm," he muttered. "This way."

We headed towards the cemetery. Soon the colossal walls and gate stood before us. The gate was wide open. It was deathly silent inside. Earl motioned for me to be quiet and we crept through the gate. Near a gravestone was an overflowing pile of fish. Earl's net lay nearby. A flashlight, propped up on a headstone, shone straight onto the fish heap. We crept closer to take a look. Click. A sudden flash of light blinded me.

"Oh. It's only you," Nick said. He put down his camera disappointed.

"What are you doing, you idiot? Mom's about to have a heart attack!" I shouted.

"No one believes me. And you chickened out," Nick shouted back. "So I had to get proof. I set a trap and I'll get a picture and then mom and dad will have to believe me. And you," he turned to Earl. "You lied. You told my dad you scared us with bear stories. You lied!"

"Yes," Earl replied softly. "Tell me about your trap."

Eager to tell someone his plan, Nick said, "I realized the sasquatch liked the fish you caught. So, I gathered the rest up with your net and brought them here. I'll hide, the sasquatch will come and I'll take a picture." Nick held up his camera. "Proof! And I found something else."

"What did you find?" Earl remained calm and composed even with Nick yelling.

"This!" Nick held up a small leather notebook, the pages yellowing, the edges worn. "I found it with your net. I know what you are. And all these dead people," he gestured to the names on the gravestones. "I know what they are too."

"What am I, Nick?"

I stayed back, afraid to approach Nick, afraid to interrupt.

"You're a liar," he said. "You protect the sasquatches and you get rid of any evidence they exist. It's all here in your book. You've been covering it up your whole life. And your entire family has been doing it for hundreds of years. I'm going to take this book and my picture and tell everyone."

"You're a clever boy Nick. And brave." Nick grinned triumphantly. Earl continued, "But what happens after that?"

"After what?"

"After you take the picture. The camera flash. What if it scares the sasquatch?"

"I'll hide in there." He pointed to the mausoleum.

"You've been touching the fish. He'll smell you out."

Nick faltered, uncertainty on his face. "I... I'll run."

"He's fast. Faster than you. He'll catch you and you don't want that."

Nick's face fell, dejected. He looked to me.

"Let's go home Nick. I don't want you to get hurt."

"But what about the sasquatch?" he said. I saw the pain in his face. "And what about him?" He pointed to Earl.

"You're right," Earl said. "I protect the sasquatches. But I also protect you. Any person who really finds a sasquatch doesn't live to tell about it."

"Well what about you?" I asked.

"We have… an arrangement. We need each other. But if I ever break the rules…" he trailed off. "Let's say he's not very forgiving. Let's go back to your parents and keep you safe."

I approached Nick and hugged him. "I won't chicken out again, ok?"

"Thanks."

Movement came from the gate. The sasquatch approached. He grunted and sniffed the air, attracted by the smell of the fish. He stood upright, paused and looked around.

"Kids you listen, you hear?" Earl whispered. We both nodded. Earl stepped in front of us, shielding us from the sasquatch's view, his hand resting on the rifle. The sasquatch saw Earl and huffed.

"I'm just leaving now big guy," Earl spoke coolly. Earl reached out his hand backing us away. The brute turned back to the fish and stepped into the light. He was the most terrible thing I ever saw. Black menacing eyes sunk deep beneath a high forehead and domed shaped skull. Dark bristly fur covered a powerful chest and arms. He could snap me in two if he wanted. He bent down to retrieve his snack.

We were almost at the gate when Nick tripped, falling backwards. The sasquatch's head swung up. The camera clattered to the ground. Click. Flash. We froze, horrified. The beast screamed, clawing at his eyes.

"RUN!" Earl shouted. "RUN AND DON'T LOOK BACK!"

"But what about you?" I cried. The same time Nick was repeating, "I'm sorry. I'm sorry. I'm sorry."

"GO NOW!"

Earl swung his gun off his shoulder just as the

sasquatch charged swinging his formidable arms. We ran. Gunshots rang out. The terrible piercing scream of the sasquatch penetrated the night. We didn't stop. We ran until we burst through our cabin door, safe.

* * *

Our overjoyed parents didn't question Nick's lie about going for a nighttime stroll. My brother and I were grief stricken and anxious. What had we done? Was Earl alive? The rest of the night remained eerily quiet. In the morning dad announced it was time to leave. We packed up our things. I kept going outside, waiting for Earl to come tell us he was all right. But he never showed.

I dragged myself into the car not wanting to leave. Dad drove up to the registration booth and rolled down the window.

"Whoa!" he said. "What happened to your face Mr. Earl?"

I jolted up in my excitement, pressing my face against the glass to get a better look. Nick jumped up next to me vying for a better view. Earl sat in the booth with his grey tufts of hair, his missing teeth and a great oozing gash down his cheek. Earl was alive!

"Oh, I had a little trouble chopping wood this morning."

"You should get that looked at," mom said, concerned.

"Will do ma'am. Thank you."

"Thanks for finding our boy last night. Thought he could go for a midnight wander." Dad shook his head. "Kids."

"You're mighty welcome." Earl drawled. He retrieved an envelope from his shirt pocket and handed it to dad. "Nick left this behind. Hope to see you again."

Mom smiled weakly. Dad nodded politely and handed the envelope to Nick. They had no intention of ever returning to The Yelping Dog. We kept our faces up to the window as dad drove away. Earl smiled and winked and gave a feeble little wave. We never saw him again.

Nick tore open the envelope. It was a photo. On the back Earl had written, Be careful how you use this. He flipped it over. A grainy, dark figure crouched over a shadowy lump. This was the picture the camera took as Nick fell. That's all? I thought. "It's so blurry. I guess if you turn it this way you can kind of make out what it is."

"Yes! Proof! It's amazing." Nick grinned, exultant.

* * *

There it is. My strange, scary, true story. The sasquatch is real and I'm lucky to be alive. He's out there somewhere lurking in the shadow of the woods. If you ever hear that terrifying, unearthly roar that sends tingles down your spine and fear into your core, run. Run as fast as you can and never go back.

Believe what you will. But Nick will tell you that sasquatches really exist and he has the proof.

THE BIG HOLE
by Joan M. Baril

"What the hell?" my father said. "Those little guys are still digging that hole." My dad, in his police uniform, had just arrived home from his shift and joined my mother, my sister and me at our kitchen window which gave a good view of the yard next door.

We all stared at the big hole, roughly coffin-shaped but much larger and deeper. Even though it was raining lightly, the two neighbouring kids had been at it for hours. Eight-year-old Andrew (Popcorn) Marrin, a square muscular red-head, knelt on the edge hoisting up a bucket of soil with the aid of a rope. After trotting a few feet to the end of the lawn, Popcorn, with a casual underhand toss, shot the contents onto a small mountain of dirt that had been growing ever larger as the summer progressed.

Over the twin poles of a ladder scrambled ten-year-old Robert (Rocky) Marrin, covered in dirt from head to runners. Like his younger brother he was built like a boxer and just as strong. He motioned with his thumb for Popcorn to take his place in the hole and in a few seconds the bucket sequence recommenced.

"One of these days," my sister said, "the sides of that hole are going to collapse and those kids are going to be buried." Her voice held a happy note of anticipation, which she could not suppress. When my father glared at her, she changed her tone. "Why doesn't their mother stop

77

them? Isn't that a parent's responsibility, the safety of the little ones?"

My father frowned. "I did have a word with Elizabeth," he said, "and she told me that children need the creative benefits of imaginative outdoor play for proper intellectual and physical development." He paused. "Whatever the hell that means."

Our neighbour, Elizabeth Marrin, had been a child psychologist who believed in giving children absolute freedom, unencumbered by rules. She explained this to me many times when I went there to babysit. I could only nod, but I wondered how she could ignore the boys' wild behaviour while at the same time imposing strange house rules including a strict vegetarian diet.

My mother shook her head. "She's a lovely bonnie lassie," she said, "and as soft-headed as yesterday's haggis. Too bad the father's not around to set those wee imps straight. As for this digging mania, something set them off, I'll be bound. They've been at it every day for a month."

I winced. I knew the purpose of the big hole. The boys were preparing a grave for their father if he ever showed up. They were convinced he was a vampire and were working on a plan to bury him with a stake through his heart. Unfortunately, I was responsible for the idea. Inadvertently, I had started the scheme in motion and now, I did not know how to stop it.

I was just about to confess when my mother turned to me. "Janet, ye'll have to baby-sit those lads tonight."

"Why me?" I cried. "Why always me? Why not Leanna for a change? No! I won't do it!" I was sixteen years old and too big, I thought, to be ordered around like a child but, even as I protested, I knew the outcome. There was no standing against my mother.

"Don't blether," my mother said. "You know Mrs. Marrin wants you. Not Leanna. She likes you. She pays well. She doesn't want your sister ever since she locked the boys in the hall closet. You'll go and that's it and we'll hear no more about it."

"Nyah, nyah," my sister said making a horrible face at me and sticking out her tongue. "Putting those brats in the closet was the best thing I ever did."

My sister's first baby-sitting job had not gone well. It took place last winter a few days after Elizabeth Marrin and her children moved into the small house next door. Rocky and Popcorn had pelted Leanna with Lego, leaped at her from the furniture and tried to tie her feet together. When she tried to restrain them, Popcorn bit her on the neck. That was when she lost her temper and, no weakling herself, grabbed each child by their upper arms, dragged them to the hall closet and threw them in. She put a chair under the doorknob to hold it in place. An hour later, mother Elizabeth arrived and was appalled. She released her pounding, screaming sons and cuddled them to her as she rounded on my sister who did not hang around but shot out the door for home.

Ever since, I was the baby sitter of choice.

I always prepared well for my baby-sitting stints. When I arrived, the boys threw themselves on me, smiling and hugging. As soon as their mother was out the door, Popcorn whispered, "Did you bring the candy?"

I nodded.

"And Elvis?"

I nodded again.

"We sure as hell love you, Janet," Rocky said.

"Yes, we do," Popcorn said. "We hate your sister. She locked us in the closet. Mom says we got a big trauma."

"We did," Rocky explained. "A big one. If you get traumas our mom says you get neurosises and your brain is feccted and you grow up to be mentally diffident. You walk all bent over with your hands touching the ground." He illustrated by doing the gorilla walk around the room.

"Your mother is so right," I said, glancing out the front window to make sure Elizabeth Marrin's blue Datsun was gone. "First Elvis," I said, "but remember, Elvis is worth

79

three candies and if there's any messing up the room you lose two." I took the box of Smarties out of my pocket and held it on high. The boys' wide eyes followed the box as I shook it in the air. Their mother did not allow candy or sweets of any sort. A few Smarties brought them to heel brilliantly.

My 8-track tape player, hidden in my big purse, was useful because Elizabeth Marrin banned rock and roll from the house. TV was also forbidden but, as yet, I hadn't thought of a way to smuggle in my family's set. As I set up the tape player and put in the Elvis cassette, the boys were jiggling with excitement. At the first guitar chords, they began to dance wildly waving their arms. "You ain't nuttin' but a hound dog," they yelled. The house shook but I stood ready to prevent any damage. In the middle of an aerial summersault, Popcorn's arm hit the standing lamp. I grabbed it just in time.

"Two candies off," I yelled.

"No-o-o," Popcorn wailed and threw himself on the chesterfield. But he knew I would not relent. Once, during a pervious baby-sitting occasion, the boy, angered by the penalty, threw himself on me, and bit my arm. Even as I felt his sharp teeth sink into the area above my wrist, I managed to grab him and slam him into a chair. Holding him in place by the shoulders and avoiding the kicking legs, I explained that, if he ever bit me again, I would tell my father, who was a policeman, and he would go to jail. That was the end of the biting.

So far.

But I was always on my guard.

Both Popcorn and Rocky had met the police before although not my father directly. A few weeks after they arrived in Port Arthur, they had emptied out all the gas from the gas pump in the yard of the Ontario Ministry of Natural Resources at the end of our street. They also released the pedigree poodle in the next block from its cage, put there because it was in heat. The dog was lost for two days. Each time they'd been let off with a warning. But now, a rumour was going around that they picked up cigarette butts, removed the tobacco, put it in an old pipe and collected five cents for five puffs from the kids in the neigbourhood. When I questioned them, they denied it strenuously.

The Elvis tape ended and the two collapsed on the rug. I doled out the Smarties, three for Rocky but only one for Popcorn. I did not allow a choice of colours. The boys regarded the candies gravely as if they were precious gems, turning then over, admiring them and, after slowly licking the hard coating, compared the colours of their tongues. I found this disgusting, but I let them do it because it kept them quiet. Then they had to wash their hands and faces, brush their teeth and put on their pyjamas. These tasks were worth two Smarties each and were done quickly.

They snuggled down beside me on the couch ready for their comic book and goodnight story. Little drops of water clung to their fuzzy red brush-cut heads. Their smiles were wide and innocent. They smelled of soap, toothpaste and Smarties. Their hard square bodies leaned against me as they regarded the new comic with happy anticipation.

"Superman today," I said as I unrolled the magazine and showed them the cover. Comics were forbidden in the Marrin household so both boys stayed close as I read the entire thing through. Because they sat quietly without roughhousing, kicking me or punching, they each earned their reward of two Smarties.

"Time for bed. But first your bedtime story."

It was at this stage, during my first session as a babysitter last winter that I made my big mistake. I had planned to tell stories from Canadian history, to give them at least something of value. So I'd said, "I'll tell you the story of Laura Secord."

"We know Laura Secord," Popcorn had said. "Her picture's in the school. She had a stupid cow."

"She saved Canada," I said.

"Boring." said Rocky. "Why did she take the cow with her anyway?" He slipped off the couch to go who knew where.

"But," I said, thinking fast, "What you don't know is that Laura Secord was a vampire."

"A what?" he said. He climbed back up beside me.

"Yes," I said quickly explaining what a vampire was. I described Laura's pointed teeth her staring eyes, her lust for blood. I explained that she stayed in the cabin all day because one beam of sunlight would kill her. That was why she did not run away when the American soldiers came. But when night arrived, she said she had to milk the cow. Then, she took the animal with her on her sixteen-mile-trek so she could drink its blood.

The boys nodded. It all made sense to them.

I spun out the story as long as possible, heading for the big finish when Laura reached the Canadian troops before the sun came up, delivered her message and ran off to spend the day in a cave. I described the next night when she went back to the cabin and released her husband, who was also a vampire. The couple pounced on the American soldiers who had fallen asleep. Later they threw the desiccated bodies into the Niagara River where they went over the falls and were never seen again.

Popcorn and Rocky were so enthralled, I hated to break the spell. I added the little known fact that Laura and her husband, now heroes, lived on for many years until the villagers discovered they were vampires and killed them. I described in detail how the angry neighbours ran stakes through their hearts and buried them in a deep coffin-shaped grave.

"That was one hell of a great story," said Rocky, accepting his candy reward. That night, as I walked them into their shared bedroom, I felt bad for filling their innocent minds with such tripe.

"We had one damn big trauma today," Rocky said as

he climbed into bed. "The biggest."

"What?" I said,

"Our father is coming back to live with us. We don't like him. He has a giant neurosis."

"He gives me traumas," Popcorn said. "I'll grow up an idiot. Or maybe a moron." He jumped up and started to punch the quilted headboard of his bed. "Pow! Pow!" I let him punch because the thing was in shreds anyway.

"When's he coming?" I said.

"We don't know," Rocky said. "Mom doesn't know a damn thing."

"Who told you he was coming?"

"Some big kids up the street."

"Do you believe that?"

"Damn right," said Rocky. "When we were little he always came back until Mom made him go away again."

As I tucked them in, and counted out two Smarties each to eat in bed, I assured them that the big kids were playing a joke but they looked skeptical. They could now read for half an hour in bed before I turned out the light. Their mother had started this practice and I continued it with one difference. The half-hour read was worth five Smarties but any roughhousing and all would be forfeit. As I closed the bedroom door, I heard them whispering excitedly to each other. When I came back thirty minutes later, Rocky said, "We've got it figured out. Our dad is a vampire."

"What? I don't get it. That's silly. It's just a story," I doled out the last candies.

But just before I turned off the light, I heard Rocky say to his brother, "Don't worry, Popcorn. We'll be ready for him."

I regretted that story then and regretted it more later when I saw them digging the hole and guessed what was in their minds. But I did nothing because weeks went by and the absent dad never showed up. The gossip at Port Arthur Collegiate claimed Elizabeth Marrin had separated from her husband, returning to live in her hometown. Her rich father, who owned a lumber company, bought her the house and paid her a generous allowance. No one knew why the marriage broke up but I reasoned that Elizabeth, so softhearted and scatty, probably put up with a lot before she left him. I believed it was unlikely that he would ever turn up in Port Arthur, not with her powerful father around.

My more immediate problem, I felt, was I had hooked them on gore. After the Laura Secord session, they demanded more Canadian history. With the help of the horror comics sold at the corner store, I was able to think up a variety of plots: David (Frankenstein) Thompson; Prime Minister Mackenzie Zombie King; Suzanna Moodie, Werewolf of the Bush and so on.

"The story tonight is about John A. Macdonald," I said settling back on the chesterfield.

"Canada's first Prime Minister," Rocky said. "We studied him in school. Our father said he was a drunk."

"Yes," I said, "but the reason is this: he was dead. He was one of the living dead. Under his clothes, his body was all green and hung down in shreds. He only drank alcohol to stay in the land of the living."

The boys nodded their understanding and the story was on.

Late the next afternoon, I hurried home after choir practice to see a large station wagon in front of the Marrin house. It was parked on the small front lawn taking up most of the space. It looked more like a candidate for the wrecking yard than a workable vehicle. One of the tires was almost flat creating a severe sideways lean. The chrome was spotted and twisted and in a few places missing entirely as if someone had hacked off chunks. Deep scratches criss-crossed the wooden sides which were dark with dirt. Rust had eaten the metal all around the wheels and the bottom of the doors, and spattered dark red spots across the hood.

I wanted to peek inside the vehicle but I did not dare. Someone, maybe the returned father and husband, for the car must be his, could be watching from the house. As I walked slowly past, I noted the back bumper was held in place with rusted wire. A blackened exhaust hung underneath almost touching the ground. The back window was covered in either black paint or paper, I could not discern which. This vehicle was so ugly it would give anyone a trauma, I thought, with a pang for the boys. Their friends would tease them unmercifully.

"So the missing husband turned up," my mother said, as she was ladling out the barley soup. A large macaroni and cheese casserole sat on top of the stove. "Your dad's late. He's in court. We'll eat with him later. Your sister's at volleyball practice. So stoke yersel' up on soup and we'll have a late meal." She sat down at the table, a cup of tea in front of her.

"Did you see him?" I asked.

"Indeed I did. He walked in as if he owned the place and later carried in a few boxes. I guess he's here to stay. He's nay bargain that one. Braw looking lassie like Elizabeth sure picked a dud. Peaked little feller. Face as dour as a burnt boot. Still an all, he may keep those wee devils in line."

"How'd she meet him?" I was interested in Elizabeth's story.

"She told me once," my mother said, saucering her tea and blowing on it to cool it, "that she met him at a party when she was at university in Toronto."

"But if he was so poor," I said thinking of the station wagon, "and so bad looking, why marry him?"

My mother gave me a long strange look. "Well, I'll tell you something, Janet. A bonny rich lass attracts a certain type. The predator. I think she had to marry him after a while. At least that's what she hinted. She only said her parents insisted."

I was amazed. My mother had never talked like this

before, as if I were a grown-up. "You mean," I said, "she got," I hesitated, "pregnant?"

"Aye," my mother said. "I dinna know for sure but…" She let the rest of the sentence hang.

An unpleasant thought hit me. "Do you think he got her pregnant on purpose so she had to marry him? To get at her money?"

"Possible," my mother said. "It's been done before."

"But what made her leave him?"

"Ah, on that subject she said naught. But it could be anything. Let this be a lesson, Janet. It's a hard life for a woman if she's nae canny when chosin' a husband."

During the next week, I caught only a few glimpses of Mr. Marrin. The digging in the back yard went on as usual. On Thursday, to my surprise, Elizabeth Marrin phoned and asked if I would babysit next Saturday afternoon. When I arrived the husband was sitting at the wheel of Elizabeth's Datsun and, as soon as I got inside the house, he honked the horn and kept it up. Elizabeth, flustered, grabbed purse, rain jacket and rain hat. "I made some seaweed snacks in case we're late for dinner," she said. "And Janet, it looks like rain. If it does, will you get the washing off the line?"

I nodded.

I suggested to the boys we go to the park and they agreed. Leaving by the back door, we walked down the lane that ran beside the house toward busy Arthur Street and Waverley Park. Predictably, once there, the brothers went wild, wrestling like bear cubs on the grass, vaulting over the ornamental cannons, somersaulting down the hills and chasing each other around the war memorial. We circled my high school where they became absorbed in hunting for pieces of chalk thrown out the windows by unruly students on the last day of school. Recalling the horrible seaweed snacks waiting in the fridge, I took them down the hill to Peanut Jim's Confectionary for a persian donut and a coke.

They were in sugar bliss on the return journey so I felt it was a good time to ask questions. "How's life with your dad?"

"Trauma," said Popcorn. "We get lots. He hurts me." He pouted, kicked his feet and punched the air.

"What does he do?" I asked, my heart pounding with fear that I would hear about beatings.

"He does this," and Popcorn bent his middle finger with his thumb and then flicked it forward on his head. It made a loud snapping sound.

"Yeah," said Rocky, "the bugger flicks us. When we come out of the bathtub, he flicks us with the towel if we start horsing around. And he calls us names and says bad things."

"Such as?"

"Space Aliens. Creatures from the Black Lagoon. Spawn of the Devil. He says we'll end up living in a tarpaper shack on the Nipigon Highway."

"That is not nice," said Popcorn. "It gives me trauma. Besides he's a vampire."

"Come on," I said. "That's not funny."

"Oh yeah." Rocky was indignant. "Well, put this in your pipe and smoke it, Janet. He's got cases of blood in the car and more in the pantry. He drinks it all day long. He did the same thing long ago when we were little. Blood, blood, damned blood. All day long. Then he passes out."

We had reached the back door of the house. The washing had turned wild, billowing and dancing on the line, barely held in place by the pegs. A bruised sky glowered over us. I heard a far off noise that might have been thunder.

In the house, Popcorn opened the pantry door to show me several tall bottles of red liquid on the top shelf.

"I think it's wine," I said. "Just wine." I looked around for the clothesbasket and spied it under the kitchen table.

"He passes out," said Rocky. "I think he's in the back of the station wagon right now. I think I saw him crawl in there. He's got blankets there and he drinks blood and passes out. He pisses into an empty blood bottle."

"No, Rocky. He went off with your mother."

"No, Janet, he didn't. He didn't." Rocky clenched his fists and glowered at me. "He got out of Mom's car and walked away up the street but when she drove off, I think he came back and climbed into the back of the station wagon."

This was more than absurd. I had to check it out. Just then, the first scatter shot of rain hit the windows.

"Stay here," I said picking up the clothesbasket. "I'll get the laundry in and then we can talk about this."

The wind, now much stronger, slammed the back door behind me but not before I heard Rocky say, "Come on, Popcorn."

A summer storm in Northern Ontario is fierce and fast. I could feel the temperature dropping as the storm gathered itself over the city, setting the trees in motion and the clothes flailing. I was halfway finished, rushing, not stopping to fold anything, throwing the pins wildly into the basket as the rain tried to tear the garments from my hands when I heard the roaring, but, this time, it was not thunder. I looked behind me. The station wagon was coming down the lane, black smoke belching from its rear end. Only Rocky's eyes and bullet head showed through the steering wheel as he tried to turn the wagon. It skimmed the first clothesline pole and the platform where I was standing. A loud unsteady clatter rose from the vehicle as Rocky cranked the wheel. I had a brief glimpse of his square white face as the station wagon slithered across the back lawn, one wheel hitting the edge of the hole and then it fell in with a crash as if the monstrous thing had fallen apart, leaving only the crunch of broken glass and the screaming inside.

My father was out of our house, running in big leaps. The station wagon was half in and half out, its back end sticking straight up in the air. It was canted on one side but without enough room to fall over. Popcorn had cranked down his window and my father, with one foot on the side of the wagon, and avoiding the still spinning tires, leaned forward and yanked him out. Rocky followed. Both were wailing. Blood was running down their faces. Their clothes were awash in red liquid. I could hear sirens converging on us. Later I learned that my mother had phoned the ambulance and both the fire and police departments.

I yelled at my father. "Mr. Marrin. He may be in there."

The back door of the wagon popped open. A strange man hung above us for a second and then jumped, toppled over, gathered himself upright and scurried for the house. My dad, in two bounds, had him by the lower arm and was bending him backwards. My mother appeared, snatched up Popcorn, lifted him over her shoulder and ran with him to our place. I grabbed Rocky and dragged him after her but the ambulance guy stopped me and took him. My mother handed over Popcorn. She then pushed me toward our house.

"Are you hurt, Janet?" she said once we were inside.

"No. Just wet."

"Good, put the kettle on then. Keep the door closed. The reporters will be here and we don't want our name in the paper. Why did you leave those brats alone?"

I was stunned. Was I going to be held responsible for the entire fiasco? "I told Mrs. Marrin I would get the washing in." I felt a depressing drop in my stomach as I realized my mother would blame me unjustly but, surprisingly, she said only, "We'el, that's the end of it then. Nae doubt you knew what you were doin'. A nice cup of tea will do us both good and we can watch from the kitchen window."

A week later, my dad explained. "Ronny Marrin was well known in Toronto for making and bootlegging red wine. Things were getting hot so he closed shop, bought the station wagon, loaded it up with the stock and headed north probably selling the goods as he went. Arrived here.

We ferretted out a few of his local customers. After a little encouragement, they decided they'd testify for the Crown. So Mr. Marrin is charged with illegal selling of alcohol. Now, he's sitting behind the pipes at the Cooke Street Station. Can't make bail. But as it is, he'll not get much. A month or two. You'll see him back next door one of these fine days."

"I doubt it, Duncan," said my mother. "The old man will pay him to get going. But Elizabeth'll have no luck getting a divorce, poor creature."

"As I was saying," my father said evenly. "He may show up again. Every time he needs money."

"But the boys will get older and bigger," I said. "They may not get off with a few scrapes and cuts next time," I said. "And neither will he."

Both parents looked at me. They were frowning but nodding as if they were considering my words. "Very good, Janet," my father said. "Those lads are a force of nature, right enough. You may be right. This story is not over, not by a long shot."

But we were wrong. On Monday, Elizabeth Marrin's father showed up with a crew of lumberyard workers. By late afternoon, the station wagon was gone and the hole filled. Ronny Marrin spent only six weeks in jail. According to my dad, the old man met him outside, handed him a few bucks and told him to hit the trail. He never did return as we all expected.

Both boys, superficially cut and bruised, seemed unaffected by their experience. I continued to babysit from time to time for the next three years. As they got older, they became quieter as if their excess energy had drained into the big hole along with the station wagon. Surprisingly, Elizabeth got her divorce, married again and moved to Winnipeg. We lost track of the family completely. Years later I heard both brothers had been brilliant high school students and star football players. Later still, I learned Popcorn became an engineer and

Rocky had started a branch of his grandfather's lumber business in Kenora. They both married, had children.

"That accident traumatized those kids, teaching them a much needed lesson which made them see the error of their wild ways," my sister said. This was her favourite theory, which she repeated every time the subject of the Marrin family came up.

But I had my own idea. Maybe Mr. Marrin was a sort of vampire, who in Toronto, attempted to suck the life force out of Elizabeth and her children, turning up drunk and unpleasant until she gave him money. Had he repeated the performance many times until she fled? Did he have the same plan in mind when he showed up again in Port Arthur? If this was the case, the brothers had done a good day's work. Even though they were very young at the time, I believe they understood this very well.

MAYFLY
by Sara Mang

Ambulances come around these parts for a heart that stops or a hip that breaks, but never for a little girl's leg that's been gnawed to the bone by a rabid dog. There are the days, of course when Ms. Geraldine calls the ambulance complaining about tightness in her chest, when really her design is to get a free trip to St. John's. She hobbles out to the ambulance, nails painted the same glossy shade as her handbag, leaning on the paramedics, shaking her head back and forth like she's in a bad way. In a day or two, she's back in Rourkney Bay, spry as spring with a new shade of mauve in her hair.

Easter Cove Hill is the only way into Rourkney Bay from the city and the sirens are audible before the ambulance appears. It accelerates down the hill and across the bridge and past the only store, Young's Grocery and Gas. It passes the part of town we call The Flats - low, muddy ground that surrounds a number of grassy fields where horses and sheep graze. When the tide comes in, the saltwater fills the low ground, stranding the sheep and the horses on the grassy patches that become islands until the tide changes again. Once over the bridge, the ambulance rumbles down a few rugged lanes to one of the one hundred and seventy-eight houses that make up this town where news of an ambulance is delivered at hurricane speed.

Ten year-old Sophia came to town with her mother, Liz McCarthy last spring. Ms. McCarthy got a job at the new inn, The Rourkney Bay Inn to be precise. Don't even think of calling it a hotel or a motel, because it's an inn, the likes of which have never been seen around these parts before. A young lady from Rourkney Bay, Ms. Nita Hobbs, went up to Toronto years ago, made her fortune and came back to build this inn. It doesn't look like an inn. It looks like a couple of rectangular boxes, full of windows and perched on stilts, hanging over the ocean like a beacon. Ms. Hobbs had a fellow from Sweden or someplace design the blueprint but everything else about it comes from Newfoundland. Many folks can't see why she didn't get someone from here to plan out the place. We've been building houses on the coast for generations and we know full well how to build things that can withstand whatever weather the ocean conjures. But she wanted this Scandinavian fellow and it's her choice. It's her inn, after all and she did the right thing because the shape of it and those stilts have people talking and writing about it in all kinds of fancy architectural and design magazines.

Now, I'm not concerned with these types of magazines, I'm well into my easy years and the design of my little square house is as complex as need be. But Rourkney Bay and its new inn have been all over the news. It costs over a thousand dollars to stay for one night, for God's sake. Ms. Nita Hobbs has people from all over the island making quilts and building furniture and preparing the meals of lamb and scallops and dandelions. Everything is topnotch with the savoury flare of Newfoundland, I gather. I can understand why her design has made headlines, and I'm glad of it. Rustic, they call it. Rustic is all the rage nowadays. Rustic. I can tell you a thing or two about rustic.

Sophia's mother, Liz, is an artist from Labrador. Now, Liz is not her real mother, mind you, she's her foster parent, bless her heart. She's been commissioned to build light fixtures for the inn and she's doing it out of fishing line. I haven't seen them myself but people use words like peculiar, minimalistic and modern to describe their aesthetic. Most of us here in Rourkey Bay are antiques, one might say. There are a handful of younger families, maybe five or six, who make do with seasonal work. Usually they leave for a few months at a time to work elsewhere. It's a pretty simple life here in this remote little fishing village and you can get by just fine without buckets of money. One of the young families is Nora and Reg Nash. She's a school teacher and the mayor and he's a carpenter. He's been doing some work at the inn as well. They have a little girl, Tessa who is also ten years of age. She is the sweetest little thing, not much talk, but as even-keeled as they come. Before Sophia came to town, there were no other little girls so Tessa would come here for visits most days. I always have fresh bread and molasses.

"Ms. Rose, there's a new girl moved in next door. She has curly hair that is mostly tangles." Tessa was sitting on the bench, her two hands tucked under her bottom. I fixed her a glass of lemonade with ice and a substantial slice of warm homemade bread, blanketed in molasses.

"Is that so? Curly hair, like your curly hair Tessa?"

"Curlier, and it bounces. Her perfume smells like the priest's incense. Yesterday, we were in her front yard looking for sow bugs and she stood up and put her hands on her hips and looked out over the Flats like she was staring at a painting on the wall." Tessa hunched over her plate and took a monstrous bite of bread.

"And does she like it here? She's a foster child you know and I hear she's lived in Labrador and St. John's mostly." Tessa continued to chew her bread, nodding her head, her mouth full.

"Yeah, she's had six mothers. I guess she likes it here. She wants to ride the horses on the Flats and she loves the way the chickens and the dogs run around all over the

95

place. She says the chickens look like they're in a rush."

"Now don't you torment those chickens and for God's sake keep clear of the horses. They're as wild as the wind. You can't ride them."

"I think she will Ms. Rose."

"Are you going to show her your bugs?"

"No."

Each and every speck of Tessa is caution to the brim. My God, she is tentative. She thinks twice about every move she makes. Her eyes are too big for her face because they get so much exercise, darting around the way they do. She is probably a few inches taller than she presents because her scrawny frame is forever hunched. Her shoulders hoisted to her ears like there's a chill permeating right through her. I often think she is that way because she's grown up in the absence of other children. She plays cards and bingo with the rest of us, never making so much as a peep out of turn. She plants potatoes and onions and turnip with her mother and puts salt and pepper on her boiled greens. Like a genuine little Molly Maid, she hangs clothes on the line, holding a clothespin between her lips. I'll often see Tessa and her father walking up the hill to their barn where they keep a few sheep and chickens. The two of them in coveralls and rubber boots, shovels braced across their shoulders, a forward leaning gait. She'll shovel the manure with her father for hours. She seems to take comfort in working, which is singular for a child her age. She has no beefs about it though; never a squawk out of her. I suppose the work and its repetition transgresses her bashful nature. Now if you ask her something off the cuff like what music she likes, she clams up faster than fog. Nora often brings me one of her loaves, partridgeberry or blueberry.

"Thanks for spending time with Tessa, Ms. Rose."

"Oh, she's a charm."

"Does she talk to you much?"

"Well, yes…mostly she listens. She certainly has her

favourite stories. She always wants to hear of Old John Joe Bison who used to dress up in a pink flannel nightgown and sit in his rocking chair up on the hill. He'd pick the foggiest of nights and rock in his chair for a few hours with his legs crossed until the whole town was talking about the Ghost of Easter Cove Hill."

Poor Nora is tormented. She is tormented by her job at the school and her role as mayor and most of all, by Tessa. She works hard and she worries about everything and her torment makes a deep cleft between her eyebrows. It is awfully deep for a woman her age.

The Rourkey Bay Inn infused this town with a frenzy without disrupting the order of things. The inn was built at sea level, right below Easter Cove Hill. You can see it from most places in town and during the two years of its construction, it was hard to have a conversation that didn't include a nugget of inn trivia: They invented their own way of catching cod called cod pots. She's re-deployed the boat builders to build the furniture. Picnic tables and benches migrated to afford a better view of the inn. It wasn't uncommon to see the NTV van circulating town for newsworthy stories surrounding the inn, or for some quirky indication of rural outport living, and the people of Rourkney Bay delivered. John and Helena Careen covered their front lawn with wood carvings and suggestive whirligigs. Mostly little wooden men with little wooden penises and little wooden women with dresses that went up, and some beavers with tails that hammered like ninjas. Shameful is what it was. Arnold Pigeon acquired dozens of moose antlers from his shed and erected them on his property, adorning each antler with one of his wife's elegant bird feeders. May Lennon started painting rocks. She painted fishing scenes, colourful row houses, gawking animals, smiling flowers, bees and birds. Whatever you could think of she painted on rocks of all sizes and displayed them on her fence and around her yard, making her little yellow house and surroundings look like it was prepared for a float in the Christmas parade. Mr. Crawley, our very own centurion, stopped by my front door most days during his walk and kept me abreast of any new community efforts to secure its relevancy.

"The crowd here is gone mad, wantin' to get on the news, Jesus Mary and saint Joseph. Lisa English has more gardenias in her front yard than Buckingham Palace. Phil Downy got his grant to build a cranberry farm out the road. What's he building out there a Mosque?"

Tessa has a peculiar hobby that would make the front page had she mentioned it to anyone besides her parents (and me of course). She has a bug collection that she is very passionate about. That's what they're calling it nowadays, passion. Tessa is very passionate about her bugs.

"It's a mayfly Ms. Rose." She carried the little storage box in her two hands like it was a morsel of rainbow.

"Well now. Where in the name of God did you get that?"

"Dad took me troutin' up Rourke River and the mayflies were everywhere so I caught a few. It took me a few times but I was able to pin this one and slip it into its storage box."

"You did all that?"

"I did. Mom helped me order stuff online."

"Well…"

"The immature nymphs can live for years in the water but as soon as they mature, and grow wings, they die."

"Oh?"

"Their only role is to reproduce and lay eggs back into the water, and then they die. They don't even have mouths to eat."

Tessa continues to collect different sorts of bugs. She creeps around her yard after dark with her flashlight and insect net, crouching down in the grass like a lone wolf. Reg built display shelves in their basement where she keeps her tiny boxes of bugs neatly organized and labelled.

The more luminous species have their own lamps so that the hues of wings or thoraxes or eyes can be suitably appreciated. Tessa is strict about not having any repetition in her collection. If one of her nets or traps catches an insect that she has already preserved, she sets it free, gently whispering words of encouragement: 'hello to your queen, little bee' or 'sing, sing, little cricket.' The dragonflies are her favourite and she keeps small piles of carrot peels and fresh fruit around her yard to feed them.

After Sophia moved to town, it was rare to catch Tessa without her. They stopped in here most days looking for a snack.

"The tide was low today and we were able to go way out on the rocks where all the starfish are. You should have seen the starfish. I wanted to take some home but Tessie wouldn't let me."

"They need saltwater or they'll perish."

It was nice to see Tessa with a little girl her own age, but I missed her solo visits. It was hard to get a word in with Sophia. Tessa sat and devoured her bread and molasses quietly while Sophia delivered a monologue of their most recent adventure. Tessa was content to observe the show. And a show it was. Sophia's entire face smiled. Her eyes, her cheeks, even her eyebrows were full of smile. Her curly hair, a matted, contorted mess flopped about her face demanding full attention. She was a pleaser - her enthusiasm, contagious but excessive, her flattery, genuine but lavish. She seemed pressed for time, acutely aware that opportunities to make impressions were numbered.

"So Tessa, did you spend much time in the water?"

"We did. We were swimming for a good spell. The water's not cold at all, and I'm going by Tessie now."

"Oh?"

"We're heading to the Flats. You ready Tessie?" Tessa said thank you for the bread and they were off like krill.

"Be careful of them horses for God's sake," I yelled after them.

Truth be told, Tessa's ability to fade into the background should come as no surprise. Her father's family is like that. A reticent lot, those Nash's. Each new generation, more self-contained than the one before it. Ms. Rita, Tessa's grandmother, was well into her eighties but still kept two cows and made her own butter and cream. For over three decades, she was the community nurse but after she retired, she didn't stir far from her front step except to go to church or to the community hall when a scattered show passed through town. A few summers ago, a group performed the play Nurse Bennett about the legendary English nurse who came to work in the Newfoundland outports in the 1920s. What a production! With four actors, a pile of white sheets and a few benches and chairs, they delivered five thousand babies, extracted three thousand teeth and saved Nurse Bennet's brother in law's foot from the teeth of a lumber saw. They hauled a sled across the ice to tend to a mother of nine who had scarlet fever. After the show, the audience collected to compare Nurse Bennett's attributes to those of our very own legend, Ms. Rita Nash, aka Nurse Nash. One would think Ms. Rita would stick around for a bit of flattery but she bolted out of that hall as fast as her arthritic hips would take her.

"Ms. Rose, tell us the story of the Terra Nova Matadora!"

"The Terra Nova Matadora? Why do you love that one so much Tessa, Tessie?"

"I don't know. Tell us!"

"Carolyn Hayward, Carol, we called her, was wild. After lights out at our girl's residence in St. John's, she'd wait and wait until the creeks in the floor were quiet, then she'd stuff pillows under her blankets and sneak out the window." Tessa looked at Sophia.

"Tell her how she got out of the window. Wasn't your room up on the second floor?" Tessa knew every beat of this story by heart.

"Nobody knew how she did it. There was no ladder. She somehow got down to the street and before morning, she was back in her bed. The rest of us girls wouldn't dream of doing some of the stuff she got away with."

Sophia asked, "So how did she become a bullfighter? Was there bullfighting in St. John's back then?"

"God help me, no. There was no bullfighting in St. John's," I chuckled. "At that girl's school, Bishop's Spencer College it was called, we weren't even allowed to run. We weren't allowed to chew gum or wear makeup or cross our legs"

"Cross your legs? Why not?" Sophia asked.

"It wasn't considered ladylike, child."

"That's weird. So where did she do the bullfighting? Mexico?" Sophia seemed unconvinced.

"It was in Spain. She went there when she was twenty and fell in love with bullfighting and decided that she wanted to do it."

"Ms. Rose, is this a true story? Really?" Sophia stood up and crossed her arms. I thought she could use a few tips on being ladylike.

"As true as the day is long. Carol Hayward became a bullfighter. She came to visit me a few years ago. She's long retired from bullfighting now, of course. She lives in Peru."

"Ms. Carolyn Hayward is her name, the Terra Nova Matadora!" Tessa jumped up and grabbed a dish cloth, swiping it around her like a cape. "I'd like to be a bullfighter."

"You Tessie? You'd kill a bull?"

"Of course not. I'd just dodge it with my red cape like this." Tessa pranced around my kitchen lunging and whipping the cloth.

"Tessie, in bullfighting, the bull is stabbed and killed."

Tessa stopped her dance and stared at Sophia. "No it's not, Sophia. It just runs around after the matador. Why would they kill a bull?"

Sophia looked at me like we shared a secret. "Ms. Rose, tell her."

"Well, Tessie, bullfighting does involve killing the bull. There's a sequence of passes and rituals and finally, the bull is killed." Tessa's eyes searched the corners of my kitchen as if the answers to her confusion were hidden there.

"So did the Terra Nova Matadora ever kill a bull?" Tessa asked hopefully.

"She did kill them Tessa. That was a part of the ceremony." I didn't mention that Carol had killed over one hundred and fifty bulls. I figured I could spare her that detail.

"You kill bugs, what's the difference? We should get Ms. Carol to come to Rourkney Bay to kill off those coyotes that are spreading rabies to Mr. Henry's sheep. I'd love to meet her. A girl bullfighter. Amazing."

"Now Sophia, the men are keeping the coyotes under control. Carol didn't go around killing animals. She was very passionate about bullfighting. It is a highly celebrated event in Spain."

"I know, Ms. Rose. In my last family, my mother let me watch the movie The Bullfighter."

"The Bullfighter? At your age?"

"Oh, they let us watch rated R movies all the time. One night we had a big bonfire in the backyard to burn all of the mattresses in the house because they had bugs in them. My foster parents set up a big huge screen on a sheet in the backyard and we watched the movie Monster."

"Killing bugs isn't like killing a big bull. I collect bugs because they are…remarkable."

"Tessie, it's the same thing. Matadors think the bulls are remarkable. They collect their kills. You love bugs. Bullfighters love bulls. How is it different?"

"I don't know. Seems different I guess. I try not to hurt my bugs…."

"Anyway, who cares? Let's go to the beach."

"Ok let's go then. Coming Ms. Rose? Mom and Dad are down there. Have you seen the iceberg yet?"

"I'll be down shortly." I had a few loaves of bread in the oven. "So you've let Sophia in on your secret collection I see?"

"Yes. She thinks I should make sketches of them so I have started a sketchbook.

It had been a few summers since an iceberg of note meandered off the coast of Rourkney Bay but this one was worth the wait. Heavens, it was rectangular but with so many facets and angles that the sun had no trouble finding a platform on which to glisten. The blue green copper was magnificent. And it was terribly close to the shore. Some suspected it might run aground and park for a few weeks which has happened in the past. That day, the iceberg sat across from the inn. You could see its reflection in the windows.

The sequence of events on the day of the accident have been discussed and dissected from so many perspectives that I struggle with what is memory and what is story. The crowd collected on the beach, minding their footing as they walked across the rocks to get to the sand. Ms. Geraldine brought her mother down in her wheelchair and a few of the men ran to her, hoisting old Ms. Powell, wheelchair and all, over the rocks, like she was the Queen of Sheba perched on a litter. Mr. Crawley made his way down the beach path with his cane. He looked down at his feet, took a few steps, looked up and marvelled, then took a few more steps. Tessa and Sophia were as close to the water as they could be without getting wet, dodging the waves as they rolled. Liz McCarthy discussed the opening night of the restaurant at the inn which was happening on the following Sunday. She hoped the iceberg would stay put, making a splendid backdrop for her fishnet chandeliers. Some of the younger men, including Reg, slung their shotguns and walked to the east side of the beach where they would fire shots at the iceberg in an attempt to get a few sections to crumble. The crowd on the beach grew anxious, awaiting what was meant to be the spectacle of the summer - the great iceberg crumbling into the Atlantic.

Things fell apart in a different sort of way. Sophia held a piece of driftwood that was as long as she was tall. She kicked off her flip flops, ran into the water and threw the driftwood ahead of her, pulling herself onto it and paddling with her hands. It was then that I saw the dog. Darting down the rocky cliff on the west side of the beach, loose rocks and gravel cascading in its wake. The dog sprinted toward us, kicking up sand, head charging, white froth spilling from its jaw. Sophia also saw the dog and started to scream. Piercing screams that sustained as she fumbled and fell off the driftwood, treading her way out of the water. In full force, the dog charged her. Knocking her down, it seized her leg above the knee, locked its jaw and shook her like she was a plastic doll, her curly little mop of hair thrown about in a mess of water and mud and blood and Liz screaming and screaming. The men ran toward Sophia with their shotguns while the iceberg sailed into the Atlantic, unscathed.

By the time Sophia made it to St. John's, her mangled leg was beyond repair and was amputated above the knee. Tessa and her parents stayed in the city with Liz and Sophia for almost two months.

During their first week home, Tessa came by with Sophia in the wheelchair. Sophia was in surprisingly good spirits. She was something else, that child.

"I'm going to St. John's next week to get fitted for a prosthesis, Ms. Rose."

"That will be grand Sophia. They've come a long way with those things."

"I'm going to be so fast, and I'm still going to ride those horses on the Flats. I want to more than ever now."

"Now you stay away from those horses Sophia. They're wild and not used to being around people. They could trample you for God's sake. Tessa, Tessie, you make sure you stay away from those horses." Tessa stared out the window. She was pale.

"I think I'll go back to Tessa. I like Tessa better than Tessie."

The following week was the postponed grand opening of the restaurant at the inn. The event brought a lot of unfamiliar traffic to town. Old Mr. Crowley informed me that the Minister of Tourism was attending as well as this person and that person. He knew all the names and gossip of the government crowd from St. John's. Mr. Crawley had received an invitation as the town's honourable centurion. He had a bowtie custom made in St. John's. It was navy blue with anchors and paisley and when I asked him to elaborate on the insight behind the design he said it was all about roots and being grounded. He puts on some airs when the government crowd comes from St. John's. You'd think he hailed from the gentry.

As soon as you entered the inn, you felt like you were on the edge of the earth. It was wondrous. The floor to ceiling windows ran from wall to whitewashed wall, angled out over the Atlantic. A masterpiece perched on stilts. Aromas of foraged herbs and just-caught fish leaked from the kitchen. Butter and batter and fresh fish were smells of home but experiencing them here in this space elevated their capacity to comfort and fulfil. The tide was high and the surf was meters below us, its hush cushioning every conversation that took place that evening in that space. I felt a surge of guilt for times I had thought people haughty or ostentatious when they described a room as being transcendent, blending seamlessly with its exterior. But now, this. This was extraordinary. This was transcendent. The chandeliers draped from the ceiling - geometric, floral, white. I appreciated them even more, knowing that in another life, they were fishing nets. Ms. Nita Hobbs spoke briefly with each of her guests. She would speak to me. What would I say? I would say thank you Ms. Hobbs for saving our little town. I would try to use the word resurrect. Perhaps I would bake her some of my bread. Yes, I would bake her bread. She would love my bread. I felt an urge to weep. Such a fine place as this built in little Rourkney Bay.

Ms. Hobbs tapped her glass with her fork and the crowd settled.

"I would like to welcome you all to the Rourkney Bay Inn. Here we are reminded that nature and culture are the garments of human life. The world is suffering from a plague of sameness that is killing human joy. The idea of place is disappearing. Islands are special places because they are places where dreams outlive time."

We followed her into the lounge for some special presentations. The floor to ceiling windows continued to look out over the Atlantic, unobstructed. This time though, the chandeliers had papers hanging from them. When I looked more closely, the papers had rough edges and drawings of bugs. They were Tessa's bug sketches. As I stared at her drawing of a June beetle with its green shell I saw Tessa enter the room behind the crowd. She saw the drawings. She collected them one by one and left, leaving a trail of urine on the blonde hardwood floor.

It was over a week before she visited.

"Can you tell me about your grandmother again Ms. Rose?"

"Nan?"

"Remember you said she'd just sit in her rocking chair while you and your cousins talked."

"Yes, God bless her. She loved to hear our stories. Nan had eight sons and two daughters but her four granddaughters were the light of her life. We had done so well with our careers and our marriages. She wasn't a proud woman, but we made her very proud."

"But you said one time that she didn't have friends."

"Well, with grandfather's business, she was busy and she liked her privacy. She didn't really have time for friends I suppose."

"But she was happy?"

"Oh, Tessa, back then, the crowd didn't talk about being happy. She loved her family. She was content to sit in her parlour, listening to us jabbering about whatever was pressing to us at the time."

"I don't think that Sophia is a good friend."

"Oh Tessa, Sophia thought you'd like to have your sketches on display. That's all."

"She ripped them out of my book, wrecked it."

Tessa was playing with a string that was hanging from her shirt. She pulled and it unravelled until she snapped it and flung the frayed remnants into my woodpile. "We have to stick together in place like this you know," I said.

"I know. Sophia wants everything to be on display. I don't like to be on display. And she is moody and snappy and she's grumpy sometimes."

"Tessa, Sophia needs you and she's comfortable being herself with you. She also needs the spotlight."

"Well I don't want the spotlight. The best things happen when people aren't looking. Look at Ms. Hobbs. She doesn't parade around looking for a spotlight."

"I think you'll figure it out Tessa."

"Your nan was like a mayfly. So is Ms. Hobbs. They make things better and they are quiet."

"You know something Nan used to say a lot?"

Sophia looked up from her hands.

"Nan used to say, 'It takes all kinds.'"

We sat in silence.

"Are you going to keep collecting your bugs?"

"Yes, tonight. The rare ones come out at night."

107

MURDER: IN COLDEST BLOOD
by Wayne Douglas Weedon

Finally, after almost fifty years, I confessed to my crime. I murdered someone. I now feel a sense of relief. But, the person I confessed to refuses to believe my story.

Doris laughed as she accused me of telling fibs, "You're pulling my leg. Come on tell me, you are; aren't you? You're pulling my leg. You're a kidder." With a slight hesitation, she then added, "I like a kidder, and you're such a kidder."

I looked at her intently, and as I closely scrutinised her, I was thinking to myself, "No, I am not kidding."

My whole story was true and I was relieved to finally, after all these years, get it off my chest. Despite her being a senior, at least sixty-five, and I would guess closer to seventy, Doris was very child-like, actually quite naïve. I guess it was because I could see how immature she really was that I, out of a sense of duty, felt I should educate her to the ways of the world. That's why I decided to invite her to watch 48 Hours with me. She had never heard of this television program, nor had she heard of any of my other favourite shows: Dateline, Fifth Estate or 4 Corners, all of which I regularly record and watch.

I, being a widower, and her, being a widow who recently moved into the apartment next door to me, were developing an increasingly intimate relationship. We talked together about problems we had with children and grandchildren, and a bit about our former lives.

On a Saturday morning Doris asked, "What's your plans for this evening? Are you going out?"

I replied, "No, I think I'll just stay home and catch up on Dateline."

"Dateline? What's Dateline?"

I was shocked that she wasn't familiar with this program and I questioned, "You mean; you've never heard of Dateline?"

She shook her head and I continued, "Well, it's much the same as 48 Hours, not quite like Fifth Estate though, Fifth Estate is mild compared to 48 Hours or Dateline."

Doris seemed astonished as she stated, "I've never heard of any of these programs. Are you making them up?"

I gave her a searching look as I asked, "You do watch TV, don't you?"

As if insinuating I was being flippant, she blurted out, "Well, of course! … Of course I watch TV!"

"What do you watch then? The soaps?"

"Well, sometimes I do, but I do like The Simpsons, Corner Gas, Two and a Half Men, as well as past episodes of Cheers. You know, I mostly watch the good stuff that everyone watches."

"Everyone watches? I for one don't watch any of those shows."

She seemed astounded as she asked, "What! What do you watch?"

"I told you, Dateline and things like that."

She was giving me a questioning look as she interrogated me, "Is there really such a show? You're not kidding me … are you?"

Despite not viewing her shows, I at least had heard of them, while she had no idea what I was talking about. It was obvious to me she was living a sheltered life. As I now look back on that day, I realise she had her sights on me.

After all, we were two single seniors, and the way she alluded to sex, I believe she still had a healthy appetite. Or, maybe she thought she would use sex to lure me into a relationship. Would it all end once she got her clutches into me? I wondered.

Did she finally believe me or was she trying to bring on a truce by acquiescing to my suggestion and therefore calling my bluff as she stated, "I wouldn't mind watching one of your Datelines then. You know, just to see what I'm missing. What sort of show is it?"

"These are all investigative journalism programs. They try to get to the bottom of things."

"The bottom of what?"

I was beginning to feel exacerbated as I requested, "Just come over after dinner and watch an episode."

Doris then volunteered to cook dinner and suggested we could watch an episode or two of my shows after we ate. Obviously, I realised, she was planning a romantic evening. We settled on my barbequing a couple of rib steaks along with potatoes, with two extra potatoes, so, as she proposed, she could make hash browns to have with our breakfast. Was this a suggestion that she wanted to spend the night at my place? I don't know, but she also insisted on bringing over wine and coleslaw.

During our dinner, I described how the shows I watched delved a lot into the triple lives people tended to live: their public lives, their private lives, as well as their secret lives. She was shocked when I explained how many reputable people, including religious leaders, such as priests, ministers and rabbis, often lead secret lives, and they have sometimes committed the most horrendous crimes: raping, torturing, and even murdering their victims. I explained to her how these crimes often went undetected for years because people could not believe that such pillars of the community could commit such dreadful deeds. Also, I explained, how the religious institutions, the police, and government officials often covered up these crimes.

111

These criminals frequently just moved away and were forgotten about.

Doris kept on looking at me as if she didn't believe a word I was saying. She protested, "You're not going to convince me of that."

Doris had told me she was a devout Roman Catholic. I playfully prodded her by explaining how Jesuit doctrines were Machiavellian. She had no idea what I was talking about and she didn't know who Niccolò Machiavelli was.

I then tested her on the Kennedys, a good Catholic family, as I continued, "A lot of these stories never appear in the news but some are so notorious that they cannot be overlooked. Take, for example, Ted Kennedy; he got away with murder, did he not?"

Doris almost jumped on me as she held up clenched fists and nearly screamed, "That! That was an accident!"

I was about to declare that, at the least, it was manslaughter, but I didn't want to argue. I held my tongue, but, inwardly, I laughed at Doris's naïveté. I doubted she had ever read anything in a critical manner. It was because I wanted to expose her to real life, and to get a point across, I chose for us to watch an episode of 48 Hours which I had seen about two years previously. It was about a Catholic priest, John Feit, who, after more than fifty years, apparently confessed to the brutal rape and murder of Irene Garza, a young girl and one of his parishioners. Feit, as I write this, only through the efforts of the diligent 48 Hours reporters, is sitting in a Texas gaol awaiting trial. Despite all the evidence presented on the show, Doris felt that this priest was being framed and railroaded. It was then, after a few glasses of wine, while we were discussing what we had watched, that I came out and told Doris, I too, was a murderer. I related how I had killed a man in cold blood and my crime, like John Feit's, happened almost fifty years ago. She refused to believe a word of my story.

Despite her mocking me, I told her everything as I

remembered it. I felt, after all these years, I wanted to get it off my chest. Without thinking, as she was deriding me about my ideas concerning good people committing crimes, I blurted out, "Do you think I'm a good person?"

She answered, "Of course you're a good person. You'd never hurt anyone."

I looked her straight in the eye and confessed, "I'm a killer, and if I can kill, anyone can kill."

She gave a half-laugh but, other than that, she sat in silence as I continued my tale by explaining, "Before that day, the day that changed the course of my life, murder was the last thing on my mind. To kill any animal, especially a human being, was not part of my nature. You know me, I'm a pacifist. I killed once and I'll never kill again."

Doris then seemed to become more indulgent as she quietly listened with no further intervention. Afterwards, she, feeling a little tipsy, tried changing the topic by telling me about the satisfying sex life she had enjoyed with her husband. It was obvious to me she wasn't taking me seriously. I didn't argue. I let her believe that I was a bull-shitter by simply stating that possibly I was watching too many of these shows and maybe I was beginning to imagine things, and make things up. It doesn't really matter if she believes me or not, I had told my story, and I felt like a great weight had been taken off my shoulders. I realised, deep down inside, my brutal act, throughout all these years, had bothered me.

Then, I lied to Doris. I told her I was tired and I wanted nothing but sleep. She took the extra potatoes and left, but, only after she got me to promise to be at her place, eight o'clock sharp, for bacon and eggs.

* * *

As I lay in bed, I thought back to when it all began; my crime, the murder of my best friend.

It started out like any other weekday. At the breakfast table, my wife and I were discussing about starting a family. She suggested the name Brandon.

"Brandon?" I questioned, "That's the name of a city, it's not the name one would give to a baby."

She looked up from her bowl of oatmeal, "It's getting late. We can discuss this tonight."

I had lost track of time. I rushed upstairs to get ready. I had just enough time to come back to the kitchen and iron a shirt before rushing off to work. I could hear her upstairs getting ready to leave when I scrambled out the door.

Suddenly, halfway to work, a thought came into my head. Did I forget to unplug the iron? I was certain, being in a rush herself, she would not have noticed the iron as she left the house. I knew I would be late if I went back; but I also knew, I would not be able to concentrate the rest of the day if I did not ease my mind. I turned around on the first driveway and rushed home.

As I was opening the front door, I could hear voices. Did she leave the radio on in the bedroom? She often did this. She used the radio as an alarm clock. She would let it play until she left for work, but sometimes she would forget to turn it off. When I was checking the iron, which was unplugged, I recognised her laugh. It wasn't the radio, it was her voice, and I heard a second voice.

I crept up the carpeted stairway and down the hall to our bedroom. The door was slightly ajar and, as I got closer, their voices became louder and more distinct. I furtively peaked through the narrow slit between the door and the frame. They were nude. He was on his back and she was astride him with her hips rising and falling as they both moaned and groaned. They climaxed together in a mad frenzy of jerks and screams. I stood frozen with my hand on the knob, ready to shove the door open.

Watching my wife in bed with my best friend, I imagined what would happen if I barged in. Being twice my size, he'd laugh in my face. What would she do? Would she laugh too as he ground my face into the carpet and kicked my backside? She told me she loved my intellect and my caring nature. I was the bookworm, the nerd, the studious one with thick glasses who, while growing up, was continually teased and bullied. It would be absurd if she told me she loved my body. Once or twice a month, we would have sex. It always seemed like she was putting herself out, and we always did it in the missionary position; never like they had just displayed to me; with her on top, riding him as if she was on a wild stallion.

The blood was pounding in my veins and my head ached as I fought back the tears. I needed time to think. Despite feeling like a coward, I let go of the doorknob and slowly backed away down the hallway. I stealthily descended the stairs and crept out the front door, carefully shutting it as not to make any noise. I cautiously drove away.

It took me the whole day to calm down, collect my thoughts, and come up with a game plan. I could not stand the thought of being cuckolded; but even more, I could not stand the humiliation of people knowing. I decided to bide my time until I could think of a plan. By the time I left work I had a general idea how I would proceed.

Later, when I arrived home, she was already in the kitchen preparing our supper. As I approached, I admired her shapely body, her rounded hips, and slim straight legs. From behind, I leaned over and kissed her cheek.

She jerked me aside, "Okay, that's enough, I'm busy. You want your supper, don't you?" She then added in her usual perfunctory way, "Did you have a nice day?"

I held my composure as I casually answered, "Yes, nothing going on. Geoff's on the road for a few days so the office is quiet." When I mentioned her lover's name, I watched for her to flinch, but there was no reaction. I asked in a mechanical manner, "What about you? Anything new?"

"Nothing new ever happens at the bank."

I immediately set my plan in motion, "I've decided to take up a hobby."

"Oh! What kind of hobby? Bridge? Or needlepoint maybe?"

"I'm going to learn how to shoot."

This got a reaction from her. She stopped with a carrot dangling from one hand and the peeler from the other, "Shoot? Shoot what?"

"Well, you know, wild game. Geoff is always saying he needs a hunting partner. I thought I might enjoy going after a goose, or maybe a deer."

She stared directly at me, "Have you finally cracked?"

"No, I'm serious. I think it's about time I started doing some manly things. After all, I may have a son soon and I would like to be a well-rounded example for him."

She grunted and went back to peeling carrots.

On Thursday afternoon Geoff was back in the office. Everyone, as usual, sensed his presence as soon as he walked through the door. There was no mistaking his loud amiable laugh, and his small talk, as he walked along the cubicles greeting everyone in turn. I observed him from my office, which was in the back. He, still having a youthful and athletic presence, was attractive to the secretaries. I mentally noted his appearance: ten or twelve inches taller than me, darkish blonde curly hair that always looked slightly windblown as if he had just finished a game of tennis or badminton, a youthful and friendly smile, and a continual, joyful, contagious, laugh. Life was a bowl of cherries for him. He was always smiling and joking. In all the years I have known him, I had never seen him cross. Everyone loved him.

I waited. I knew he would, as usual, stick his head into my office and ask me how things were going. Could I pull it off? I took a few deep breaths and braced myself. My head was pounding but I knew that I had to appear calm. Would he be able to tell that I knew? He turned from my secretary's desk and walked straight towards me. I smiled as he approached, "How's the trip Geoff, any sales?"

"Sales? I'll say. That new biscuit was a hit. I left a quarter-case at Lucky Ed's to give out as samples. I'm sure they could've easily given away two cases. By word of mouth, a line of customers formed and everyone was raving. Peanut butter, chocolate chips, and coconut, all in an oatmeal base. What a combination. Even the moms and dads loved them. I've got orders for fifty-six cases."

"That's great Geoff. I always said you're the best salesman."

"Not me, I'm telling you, these cookies sell themselves."

After a little more chitchat, I became serious, "Come in Geoff, close the door behind you. I want to discuss something."

This was the first time I had ever seen him with a serious look on his face. I wondered if he could suspect I knew. He sat down on the other side of my desk. I rose and walked around the desk to sit on the chair beside him. I cautiously began, "Geoff, I need your help."

As soon as I said this, he smiled and resumed his affable countenance, "Well, of course buddy, anything, anything at all. Who's my best buddy?"

"Geoff, you have always said you needed a hunting partner."

His expression became quizzical as I continued, "Geoff, I would like to start doing manly things. I want to bag a goose, and I've been thinking, possibly a deer."

He seemed astonished as he asked, "Are you serious Bud?"

I nodded my head as I answered, "Yes, I'm serious, dead serious. I want to go hunting."

He smiled and I knew then, I was safe.

I smiled back at him as I continued, "Besides hunting, I thought I might even start attending football games. You know, get into the macho things. We haven't told anyone yet, but Jan and I have been thinking about starting a family. If it's a boy I want to be a good, positive, influence on him. You know, I want him to be more than a nerd."

I could see Geoff was starting to warm up. In fact, as the conversation progressed, he got quite enthusiastic with the idea of our changing roles. It wasn't like when we were in high school. The roles were being reversed and he was now the teacher and I was the student. He insisted that we should get started right away. We agreed for him to pick me up at seven that evening and we would go to the shooting range to get started.

We had barely got into the gun club when he handed me a Cooey twenty-two; single shot, bolt-action, rifle. By the end of the evening I could name each part of the rifle and explain how they worked together. Leaning over the counter and resting the gun on sandbags, I aimed along the open sights and fired my first shot, which actually hit the target at fifty feet.

As the days went by I progressed quickly and soon he handed me a Lee-Enfield army surplus three-oh-three rifle with a three shot magazine. It was equipped with a six-power, cross-hair, scope, which Geoff had sighted in at fifty yards.

Geoff explained as he continued with his tutoring, "When I set you up, the buck will be fifty yards, give or take, so let's see how close to the bull's eye you can get."

Later, over a few beers in the lounge, he told me about the weapon he chose for me, "This rifle is not a lot of money. It's army surplus, but, if you know what you're looking for, you can get a really good, dependable, gun for the price. This one is basically right out of the box, with absolutely no wear on the rifling. I doubt if it was ever fired before I bought it. It shoots straight and accurate."

Geoff leaned closer to me, "I'm going to let you in on a little secret. If someone has the right connections, they can get hold of army ammunition. This is a decided advantage for a hunter who happens to be in the bush. By law, to hunt deer, one must use a soft-point bullet that will expand upon contact and thus ensure a good kill. However, if a soft-point bullet strikes even a small twig, it explodes, and changes direction. The result is, you miss the target. The army uses metal-jacketed bullets, which will go right through twigs and even trees. In the bush, a hunter can still hit a deer standing behind a tree. The disadvantage is that the bullet will go right through the deer and do little damage. If you hit the deer in the brain or heart, it will be a sure kill; otherwise the shot wouldn't be lethal. There would just be a tiny hole where the bullet enters and an equally tiny hole where the bullet exits."

"You told me the deer will be in a clearing so wouldn't I just stick to using a soft-point?"

Geoff explained, "I always keep some metal-jacketed ammunition just in case. Let me tell you a story. Last fall, a group of us rode into the park on horses to hunt elk. I saw a big buck in the bush behind a three-inch poplar tree. Since he was a trophy-elk, I didn't want to hit him in the head so I aimed at the section of the tree which was directly covering his heart. The metal-jacketed bullet went straight through the tree trunk, through the elk's heart, and halfway through an eight-inch poplar behind the elk. It was a good clean kill. I couldn't have done that with a soft-nosed bullet. Look, I'll set you up with some army ammunition. You may need them in the future; but for now, you'll stick with soft-nosed bullets."

Without thinking I blurted out, "Isn't it illegal to hunt in the park?"

Geoff seemed shocked, "Of course it is. That's why we go on horseback and follow an animal trail in from Pete Shumanski's yard. The park gate is miles away."

Somehow, what Geoff was telling me didn't surprise me. Even in sports, Geoff always looked for an edge to ensure that he would win. To give him that edge, Geoff was capable of doing anything he felt he could get away with. To guarantee he would get his trophy elk, he hunted in the park, where the elk thrived and grew big.

In November, when deer hunting season started, I was ready for my first buck. Geoff and I went to Pete Shumanski's wheat field, which, as I said, was adjacent to the park. Pete had already cut and combined the grain and there were stacks of square straw bales throughout the field. Also, Pete had, 'accidently', spilled a few piles of grain close to the park boundary.

The bales were piled in such a way that one could sit on one bale and rest their rifle in a space between two other bales. Thus, the hunter would be fully concealed from the bush that was on the south side of the wheat field.

Where I seated myself, when I placed my rifle between two bales, it pointed parallel to the edge of the bush. When a deer exited the bush there would be nothing between me and him.

"You won't be shooting into the bush," Geoff explained. "I'll enter the bush from behind and push the deer through the bush towards you. With the wind in my face, the deer won't be able to smell me. However, I will make some slight noises, which will cause the deer to move away from me. When a buck exits the bush, he will be right in line with your scope. He won't run since he will be more cautious than scared. He will look around and then slowly walk out. You'll have a perfect target. Shoot him in the heart. This way you'll save the head for mounting."

I watched Geoff as he walked along the west side of the bush. When he turned and disappeared along the north side of the trees, I got up and walked over to another pile of straw bales that sat a little over a hundred feet away and directly in front of the path where the deer would be exiting from the edge of the bush. I sat on one bale and placed the rifle between two other bales. As I peered through the scope I could clearly see the path running through the leafless bushes and trees. However, the straw bales completely hid me from the path.

I waited, not daring to take my eyes off the path. Suddenly, I could see a movement. A form was slowly coming towards me. It was a buck, about three years old, cautiously walking along the well-trodden path. He would take a few steps and then stop to look around, sniff the air, and cautiously move another step or two towards me. I didn't think he would be able to smell me as the wind was blowing more on my left side than on my back.

I sat motionless. I didn't dare move as I kept my eye to the scope and my finger on the trigger. As the deer took a few paces forward and then lowered his head, I could see a shadow about fifty feet behind him. As the deer and the shadow approached, the shadow became clearer; it was Geoff slowly and cautiously coming along the path. I waited. My heart began to pound and my temples pulsed.

The buck poked his head out of the bush and into the open field. He then furtively placed one hoof onto the fresh-cut stubble. The buck's form completely obscured Geoff as I continued to wait. The buck continued to sniff the air and, as he lowered his head, Geoff's face came into view. I moved the rifle up a little to have the cross hairs right between Geoff's eyes. The deer's head came up and again hid Geoff from my sight. I waited until the buck moved his head to the side. I took a second aim and then I very cautiously and deliberately squeezed the trigger. The rifle jerked upwards, and when it came back down to rest on the straw bale, I saw no sign of the buck or of Geoff. I stood up just in time to see the buck shoot back into the bush about three hundred feet from me. Geoff was out of sight.

The judge deemed it to be an unfortunate hunting accident. I was a novice hunter who, firing at the deer, did not realise that my closest and dearest friend was standing behind the deer that I was aiming at. Why did I have metal-jacketed bullets in my rifle? I explained that I did not know. Geoff had loaded the weapon for me. I told the judge I didn't know anything about ammunition and I never realised there was a difference between metal-jacketed and regular bullets. I was new at this game. Witnesses verified my statements. The judge's decision was I was not guilty in Geoff's death. He deemed it a dreadful accident.

* * *

That concludes what I told Doris. However, there is more to the story.

At the funeral, I spoke to Mavis, Geoff's wife. I told her how sorry I was and I asked for her forgiveness.

Without a word, two weeks after the funeral, my wife packed two bags and left me. I haven't seen her since. We communicated through our lawyers to finalise the divorce.

After the funeral, I visited Mavis regularly, always asking if there was anything I could do to help. She would hold my hand and tell me not to let this ruin my life. She told me how sorry she was that my wife had left me in my time of need. I asked Mavis if she would mind if I repaired her front gate which was off its hinges. She nodded yes. There were tears in her eyes.

Two years later, Mavis sold her house and moved in with me. Her three children started calling me Dad. A year after Mavis moved in, she had her fourth child, our child. It did not matter to Mavis if I was macho or not and she treated me like a king. She was quite happy to stay home, look after the children, and have dinner ready when I came home.

I began living the life I always wished for. Sometimes though, when I was in bed with Mavis, I felt a little pang of guilt as I thought back to my former wife riding Geoff in the very same bed. It was at times like that I asked myself if I really deserved what I had. Over the years though, I had no regrets, and, until now, I felt no remorse. I sometimes wondered if I was justified in what I did. Occasionally I have deliberated how my life would have turned out if I had just walked away, leaving the two lovers to do as they may. Would Geoff have left his wife for mine, or did he look upon my wife as just a fling? We'll never know.

THE INVITATION
by Michael Lalonde

"There's a new boy at school, y'know," Doris screeched over her Slurpee. "His name's Ken."

"Like I should care," I said.

She stared at me agape. "He's from Vancouver. Have you checked him out is all I'm saying?"

"No," I said, trying to sound like it wasn't a big deal. "Why? Is he good looking?"

"No shit." Doris stared at me through her cat-eye glasses, and then she laughed. Her smile made her round face rounder and, for some reason, her eyes bluer. Was that new mascara? Still in disbelief, she repeated the question. "You haven't checked him out yet?"

"I'm really not interested—"

"Because here's the thing," she went on like I hadn't said anything. "I've invited him over Friday to watch a movie with us..." Fridays were our time, just Doris and me. Best friends since grade one. We'd been through a lot: Survivors of Ms. Fitzpatrick's Handbell Choir and Mr. Van Reekum's Save-the-Salmon Project. She'd held me when we put down Coco, and I'd listened to complaints about her stepdad. She made me laugh after Josh Spiegelmann broke my heart by dancing with another girl. He'd gotten new braces and she'd said, "His mouth is bigger than his head." And I made her look at herself in the mirror and smile after Jocelyn Boyd called her a fat cow. Still, after that, I stopped sharing clothes with her.

My heart pounded when Ken came our way at school the next day. He wore bright suspenders and a purple shirt. I changed direction, but Doris grabbed my hand.

"No," I said.

Doris locked arms with me. "C'mon."

Once we got to know him, we expected something different every day, whether it was his dad's tie or his older brother's T-shirt or some thrift shop fedora. The rich kids joked and asked him if he ever wore anything new. The better dressed, the fashion Nazis as Ken called them, wondered when he would join the circus. We asked him how he felt when they teased him. He shook it off and said, "I decide what's cool."

The first time we went to his place, I noticed he looked like his dad. He had the same dark brown eyes and black hair. Skin creamy as Grandma's porcelain figures. Once, in assembly, I wedged myself between him and Doris. He smiled and rested his arm on mine. It felt slippery as river rock as I breathed in the apple-scented shampoo in his hair.

The three of us were never apart. My friends Molly and Sarah called us the 'Tri-tards'.

But things changed.

"Wanna watch me play hockey?" Ken asked, and I said sure. "But don't tell Doris," he added.

"Why not?"

Ken's gaze shifted away from me. "She doesn't think I'm very good."

"Has she seen you play?"

"No." He half looked at me. "I just want it to be you and me."

"Really?" Why did I ask that? I'd liked him all along and I couldn't believe he felt the same way.

"Yeah, really," Ken said, looking at me now and sounding more sure. "When Doris first invited me to watch that movie, I was going to tell her I had something else going on. But when I met you at school and she said you were invited too…"

I smiled and nodded my head. He wanted me to himself, and I wanted it that way too. I'd never had a boyfriend until now.

But still—Doris was my best friend.

I'd show up at his place Saturday mornings, and his dad would drive us to the games. Ken skated over to me the first time he scored a goal.

"Did you see that?" he asked me.

I smiled and waved but his father yelled, "Kenny, get back. The game's not over."

Ken's dad was okay I guess, but strict. On the way to the rink, he'd coach Ken in the car. And afterwards, and no matter how well Ken played, he'd remind him of how he could do better—and each time, Ken folded his arms and looked down.

In the latest game, his dad said he needed to try harder. Walking me home, Ken unloaded everything and finished with, "Dad thinks I can't play shit."

"That's not what he said, Ken."

"No, but it's what he meant."

We didn't say anything the rest of the way home.

I missed Doris. We'd grown up together, talked about everything, hadn't we? Boys, clothes, families—like how she had two dads and now I had none.

What had I done with my friend? We'd stopped seeing her on Friday nights, and at school made excuses not to eat lunch at the outside table with her. When she'd see us, she'd wave, but we'd pretend not to notice, and then veer in another direction. Doris got the message. She chose to sit elsewhere on the school bus, at the front—with of all people— the grade sevens.

I waited for Ken at lunchtime one Friday, in the school's inner courtyard. The last couple of days, he hadn't shown up. Then Doris appeared. She knew how I felt about him—I'd never said anything, never even hinted, but she knew; it must have been obvious to her, to Molly and Sarah, or any of the others, that he was more than just a friend to me.

"So." she said, in a casual way that reminded me of Mom. "I only see you on the bus, and then we don't even sit together—what's wrong?"

"Nothing," I said, but she didn't look convinced. "I've been busy."

"Have you…" she hesitated, "heard from Ken lately?"

What was it to her? "What d'ya mean?"

"Ooh." Her eyes widened. "I shouldn't be the one to tell you, y'know." There was a hint of a smile. "He's quit hockey and he's been getting drunk at parties."

"Oh." I crumpled my lunch bag and stood up. "I don't go to those parties. And I don't like people who do."

Doris said, "Where are you going?" as I marched away in search of Ken.

I found him in the part of the hallway the older kids reserved, the ones sent to the office every week. When he saw me, he turned away, and I pretended not to notice as I walked past the group.

I'd wondered why he spent less time with me, why he said I couldn't watch him play soccer. And when I called him that night, and told what Doris had said, he didn't deny the parties.

"Why do you go?" I asked, and waited. "…Are you—are you there?"

"Yeah," he said, sounding annoyed.

"…Well?"

"My new friends at those parties accept me for who I am. They aren't phony."

I could feel anger well up in me. "So I'm phony?"

"—Not at all. I'm just saying these guys are like me, they're not trying to impress."

"No Ken. They're nothing like you."

"What are you so upset about?"

128

"Go to hell." Did I say that? I took a deep breath.

He sighed into the phone. "I'm there already."

"Ken, I didn't mean—"

"Yep," he said above a whisper. "I can't talk. Dad wants me off the phone."

What had I done? Part of me wanted to cheer him up and invite him to my birthday party next Saturday, but my fat mouth had ruined that. He wouldn't come now, not after what I'd said, so I handed out invitations Monday to everyone, except him—and Doris.

Thursday morning a large rainbow banner attached to my locker read 'Happy 14th Mel!'

"I'm guessing that's me," I said, staring at the drawing of a skinny diva with red hair and countless freckles.

"You think?" Sarah said, sounding like there could be no doubt.

"Oops!" Molly pointed. "I think I missed a freckle."

Everyone laughed— except Doris.

I froze. Where did she come from?

She eyed the banner, then me.

"Bitch." Doris's voice struck like a club.

I wondered when it would get to this. I clenched my fists and glared at her; I was like, What's your problem?

Doris shook her head and strutted away.

"She's such a cow," Sarah said. "Why didn't you say something?"

I shrugged and then started after Doris, walking until I was far enough away from the others.

"Doris… Wait."

She stopped.

"What's wrong?" I pleaded.

"As if you don't know."

"No. I don't."

"Don't pretend."

"You don't have to be like this." The more desperate I sounded, the more distant she seemed.

Doris tilted her head and asked, "Then where's my invitation?"

"I was going to…" I said, regretting my words as they spilled out of my mouth—so lame.

"Yeah, right." She shook her head and marched away.

On the bus after school, I thought of Ken at band camp. I'd seen him about this time on Monday as I walked past him and the older kids. He'd known I hadn't invited him to my party by then; I sensed it by the way his smile disappeared and his head lowered. I wanted to say sorry for telling him to go to hell. And I just know I should've invited him, but I couldn't with those other kids around us.

Doris came onto the bus. I watched as she sat up front. I didn't want her angry with me. What was I supposed to do? As the bus jerked forward, I glued my eyes to the window and settled in for the long ride home along Baynes Sound, past the bald eagles circling over the oyster farm, and I didn't look forward, not once.

I tossed my backpack by the stairway. "Mom?"

"That you, Mel? I'm back here."

Groceries littered the kitchen counter. She had bought all the ingredients for my cake. I'd made her promise to let me help with the frosting on the big day.

She set a jug of milk in the fridge. "Everyone's called to confirm they're coming except for Doris and Ken. What's up?"

"How should I know," I said, in an angry voice. Where had that come from? I didn't realize how upset I was about Doris. Maybe I had the problem?

Mom stopped, clenching a tin of cocoa. "Come again?"

I searched inside grocery bags, pretending to look for a quick snack. I hoped she wouldn't notice my eyes. I blinked hard twice to keep back the tears, and then said, "Ken's been away at band camp."

From the corner of my eye, I saw her shake her head. "I don't know why his mom hasn't phoned."

I shrugged off her words.

"What's wrong Mel?"

I thought of Ken and Doris and my birthday. "Everything."

"You did give out all the invitations on Monday?"

"Uh huh." Of course I hadn't, but I couldn't tell her about Ken's new friends.

I wasn't going to invite him at first, but I decided to after all when I saw how sad he looked on Monday. I'd written up his invitation after school and set it on my night table for Tuesday. But I did something stupid. I forgot about his band camp leaving early the next day. I had to get it to him first thing that morning, or else he'd be gone until Friday. When I checked the night table, I couldn't believe it—the invitation was gone.

The rest is a blur. I tore apart my room but didn't find it. Then I missed the bus. Mom wasn't impressed because she wanted to prepare my room for painting. Now she had to drive me to school first. It didn't matter because when we got there, the camp bus had left.

"What about Doris?"

"Doris?" Just quit already with the questions. I backed away from the grocery bags. "I don't know."

She folded her arms and watched me in that expectant way with raised eyebrows.

"What?" I asked.

"Do you think you could call them and see if they're coming?"

"Mom," I groaned. "Ken's not home 'til tomorrow."

"Well then, talk to his mom."

I wish she'd leave it alone. "Do I have to?"

She leaned back on the counter and raised those eyebrows again. "I need to know how many to expect."

She wouldn't quit, so I went up to my room to make my calls.

131

I sat on the bed first, and stared at the phone. I hate talking to adults. They'd be like, Why haven't we heard from you in so long? I couldn't tell them the truth. I would have to say something lame like I've been busy with school. I let their phone ring four times and then hung up, and I waited ten minutes before returning downstairs.

"Mom, I called them but no one's home."

I was relieved when she told me at least I had tried. But when I was halfway back upstairs, her voice called out.

"Phone later."

I sighed. "Okay." Then I dragged my feet up each step, wishing we'd never planned this stupid party. I didn't phone anyone. Instead, I made a new invitation to give to Ken on his return from band camp the next day.

On the morning bus I sat in my usual spot. Would Doris sit with me? I waved her over, but she stayed up front. Did she see me? I walked up the aisle to sit next to her, but she slapped her hand down on the seat and shook her head.

"Oh." I felt stared at by those around us, the same way Doris must have felt at my locker. I bent over. "Now we're even."

I walked back, past the eyes. How could she be this way? What did I do? Slouched in the seat, I listened to my music and prayed we'd get to school soon. Then I'd give Ken his invitation on his return in the afternoon. At school, the driver let us out, but I sat still until Doris disappeared.

In first period Mr. G met us in front of the change room. "Grade eights. Listen up. You won't be dressing for PE today."

"Yes! No burpees!" one guy shouted, and high-fived his friend. No one liked burpees.

We huddled on the gym floor with only the whir of ceiling fans to disturb the silence. Mr. G blew his nose and cleared his throat between attempts to talk. Did he have a cold?

"Excuse me," he said, above a whisper. "I have sad news…and I'm not sure how to say this…it concerns a fellow classmate of yours—Ken."

He drank from his water bottle and then he told us.

"He has taken his life."

What did he say? It took a moment to process. But then it sunk in. It was my fault. "No. No. No," I whispered to myself. I stood up and cupped my ears as his words spun in my head. Then he came over and wrapped a firm arm around my shoulder.

"It's okay Mel," he said, and set me back down and returned to the front.

"His…family…will need our support," Mr. G continued, but his words lay in a mangled heap. As he struggled along, it seemed as if he tugged at each word careful not to disturb the next one to it.

I had questions I wanted to ask. Like, how and where did Ken kill himself? And why? Was it seeing the others get their invitations? Not likely, he only cared about himself. Kids were crying. My mind swept me away to those burpees. I wanted to trade places with Ken and let him crank out burpees for the rest of grade eight. Why did he leave me? If only I'd given him his invitation.

Mr. G said we faced a difficult day and we needed to support one another, so the best thing we could do was to try to carry on as usual. I wanted Doris here; I'm sure she needed me too. But we didn't share the same classes.

After PE, students began texting their parents.

In Science, kids too upset to go to class sat in the hallway. Outside the window in Math, I saw Sarah and Molly leave the school in tears. They hugged and their parents drove them away. And I missed Doris even more.

At lunch I found her outside behind a rose bush, shoulders slumped at our old table, alone. She looked up from her cell phone as I sat beside her.

"It's awful," I said.

133

"Uh-huh…"

"Why did he do it?"

She shook her head and set her cell phone aside, and then she wrapped her arms around me and freed my tears. Too soon she backed away and said, "I figured you'd come, y'know." She looked away.

"Did you hear more about Ken?" I asked

After an eternity she spoke. "They say he was caught drinking at band camp. The principal dropped him off at home yesterday…around noon. No one was at the house."

"What happened?"

"His dad kept a rifle …they…found him that way."

"That's horrible."

Sweetness from the roses drifted my way. Like the roses on Grandma's casket. I've never smelled roses again without thinking of her. She'd been old and sick, and at the final hospital visit, complained about having to live so long. Still, I'd had the chance to say goodbye…not like Ken. I thought of his invitation.

"Why would he hurt himself?" I asked.

Doris's head sunk between her shoulders.

It wasn't my fault. I wanted to believe that. But the last time I talked to him I'd been so mean. My eyes wandered. Past the roses, the other tables were empty. I missed the three of us at this table.

She pawed her sandwich then set it aside. "Do you remember those striped pants of his, like the ones The Who wore?"

"Yeah."

She wiped her eyes and said, "He wore weird shit to school." Then she rubbed her nose with her sleeve, and a faint smile came. "It was fun. He kept us guessing—"

"I know."

"We teased him about being short and he'd just smile," Doris said, and turned to me. "Do you remember?"

"I do." I also remembered competing with her for his attention until he smiled less at her and more at me.

Nearby, a car's door slammed; parents taking more kids away.

I thought about that scene at my locker. "Doris, why did you call me a bitch?"

"You know."

"No." I waited for a girl to walk past us. She disappeared into a van. "Really, I don't." But Doris didn't believe me. I could see it in her face. We both knew. "It's about Ken, isn't it?"

"Partly. He actually spoke to me on Monday y'know, said you didn't invite him to your party either."

"I didn't think the two of you cared." I sighed. "What else did he tell you?"

Doris looked away and said, "That you said I didn't like him anymore, that I called his friends losers." She faced me again. "He walked away." When all I could offer was a tight-lipped expression, she nodded and said, "Things have been different."

"What do you mean, different?"

"That's the other part of why I was mad." This time, she waited for someone to pass. "The three of us were friends. Then I was left alone. I wanted to get even with you. Sorry if I embarrassed you in front of your friends."

I nodded, thinking it was easy to let go, harder to be left behind. "Doris...I'm sorry I said those things."

She leaned in. "Why did you?"

Ping. She had a text message but turned off her phone.

"Jealous," I said.

She leaned further. "Why?"

I shrugged. "I shouldn't be because you're my best friend."

Doris shook her head at the sky. "Ken and I weren't close."

Around us groups of kids spoke softly among themselves. Others bent in silence, bundles of despair. Younger boys wrestled with a football. Yet another car roared away.

"That's annoying," I said.

Doris looked at me, puzzled. "What is?"

"Kids cutting class. They didn't even know him."

"They're just caught up in is all," she said, "like us."

The bell signaled the return to class.

"Are you going home?" she asked.

"No... You?"

"Me neither."

"I'll see you on the bus," she said.

That night I told Mom about Ken and she held me close.

After eating, she said, "Looks like we'll have to postpone your party."

"I know." It wasn't the time for celebrating. It was the time for forgetting. But then there was Doris. After that scene at my locker, nothing would be the same.

Mom loaded the dishwasher, and then dangled something in front of me.

"What's this?" I pretended not to know and then crossed my arms. "You went through my stuff?"

"No," she said. "When I finished painting your room this morning, it showed up behind your night table." Those familiar eyebrows took flight.

"Oh." I thought I had checked everywhere.

She handed Ken's invitation to me. "You said you gave it to him?"

"I know."

"Melanie," she hesitated, "I'm sorry to be on your case all the time, but I am your mom. Why didn't you give him an invitation?"

"I was mad at him."

"Why sweetheart, why were you mad?"

"He had all these new friends... I didn't think he'd come to my party." After talking to Doris, I knew now that I was wrong. And if I had invited him, maybe...

She nodded. "Don't you think that was for him to

136

decide?"

I stared downward. "Well, I was going to give it to him Tuesday." Then I looked up at her. "You don't trust me anymore?"

"C'mere." She wrapped me in her arms. Then just as quickly broke away, but kept her hands on my shoulders. "Why did you lie to me?"

She'd never quit as long as long as I acted this way. "I knew how much you thought of Ken and his family, and I didn't want to have to explain."

"Explain what?" Her arms fell to her sides.

"That he'd been drinking…I didn't want to get him into trouble, and I didn't want to lose him as a friend."

Mom's expression became more relaxed, as if something I'd said had finally registered. "It hurts to lose someone close," she said.

"Like Dad?"

"Uh huh. Like Dad."

I started seeing our school counselor. That was Mom's idea. Now I volunteer as a peer support student. That was mine.

I've kept Ken's invitation. The last time I looked at it, I thought of a question for Doris and found her at our old lunch table. We talked about Ken and then I asked.

"Do you want to join the peer support team?"

"What for?"

"You're a good listener."

"I'm not, y'know."

"Oh yes you are."

She nodded. "I'll think about it." Then she smiled and stood up. "I have to go." She held a shiny apple left over. "Here, you want this?" When I shook my head, she left it on the table. "I don't want it either." She waved goodbye.

A perfectly good apple. Mom wouldn't be impressed.

I picked it up and rolled it around in my fist, small and firm, not quite ready, then brought it to my nose and took in its scent. And I thought of Ken.

I ran my finger along its skin—smooth, like his. Not a blemish. Then I set it in my backpack.

Everyday I see his invitation on my night table: if only I had given it to him. I can't part with it, not yet, nor with his shame of being sent home, greeted only by the pain of an empty house and a loaded gun.

THE LONG RIDE
by Vicki Lockwood

Paddy leaned on the gate in the long grass, removing his cap to enjoy the warmth of the morning sun on his shiny tanned head. Leaning against the rail fence, he watched the cattle trudging out into the field, satisfied after having been emptied of their milky burden. Some of them were lowing gently as they plodded through the soft pasture. Paddy inhaled deeply the scents of fresh dewy grass drying in the sun, and his nose crinkled at the other familiar odor of manure. As the last cow sauntered past, Paddy straightened up and slid the wheeled gate across, then heading away from the pasture. His black rubber boots squished through the mud of the laneway as he slowly and reluctantly headed for the house. Today would be a long and difficult day, one he had not been looking forward to. His heart ached with the loss of his precious Madge who had been his companion for the past fifty years, raising their children right here on his farm in southern Alberta. Farming was all he knew but it had been very difficult lately handling this all on his own.

He paused by the back porch to consider the old style upright bicycle leaning there. Rust was starting to form around the spokes, but the tire rubber was new. He had given the frame a fresh coat of red paint, and had taken apart and soaked the mechanisms in Varsol, oiling them before he carefully put everything back together. He had

139

replaced some of the brake parts and the handlebars. Elbow grease and chrome polish had done wonders for the fenders and even though they were slightly dented in spots, there was a definite sparkle to them. Paddy was proud of the difference his loving care had made to the appearance of the bike. It looked almost new! "You love that thing more than you love me," Madge had said. Paddy, who was a man of few words, had grunted "ahumph", but now he hoped she had known that wasn't true.

Paddy pushed up his glasses and clomped up the back steps to the porch room. Out of habit he left his muddy boots on the boot tray in the doorway and headed for the large porcelain sink to wash his hands. The house was uncomfortably silent today, except for the splash of warm water in the sink as he washed. Stepping up into the kitchen, Paddy almost expected to see Madge at the sink, wearing her favorite floral shirt dress with an apron tied around it, leaning in and scrubbing potatoes or husking corn. She would turn and smile, give him a quick peck on the cheek, and say to him "change those dirty clothes before you sit down at the table". Smiling and stealing a kiss on the lips, he would head down the hallway to do as he was told.

Now Paddy stood in the kitchen, looking at the dirty dishes piled in the sink, a mouldy loaf of store-bought bread on the table, and crumbs strewn everywhere. Tears stung his eyes as he thought about the things that used to fill his life - aromas of roasting meats and freshly baking pies and breads, and the screams of children playing on the front porch or on the lawn in the sun with their golden heads ducking and bobbing in the breeze. Paddy cleared his throat as if to clear away the loneliness; the sound echoing in the empty room. Madge's smiling face greeted him from a framed photograph on the phone desk by the refrigerator. He smiled back at her, wiping away a stray tear. The newspaper clipping on the bulletin board above

140

the phone desk caught his eye. Stepping closer, he peeked under his glasses, confirming the service was at 2:00. He had to be there on time. She would never have tolerated tardiness. Summoning up a little extra determination, he headed down the hallway to take a shower.

Once cleaned up and dressed, his fringe of salt & pepper hair neatly combed and glasses polished, Paddy carefully folded his Sunday best suit and tie and stuffed them into his worn grey backpack. Carrying the pack, he quickly headed down the hall, through the kitchen and into the mud room. He put his dress shoes into a plastic grocery bag and stuffed them into the pack as well. Then, shrugging on his rain jacket – just in case – and fastening his bike helmet under his chin, he stepped into his rubber boots. Exiting through the back door and standing on the back stoop, he slung the backpack over his shoulder. He paused to consider the faded grey Buick in the laneway. Paddy had always kept it clean for Madge, but had not driven it since her passing. He also hadn't told anyone that he had failed his bi-annual license renewal while she was in the hospital.

"It's too nice out for that old thing anyway" he thought, and with an exaggerated spring in his step, he grabbed a fluorescent construction vest off the hook beside the door and put it on over his jacket and backpack. Smiling to himself and grateful for the warmth of the day, he mounted his shiny red bicycle.

It was a tough struggle down the muddy laneway, past the cow pasture, and onto the gravel road that ran across the front of his property; especially at the snail's pace at which he was moving. Paddy was familiar with the vibrations of the handlebars, and the feel of the new rubber once he reached the gravel roadway. He picked his way, trying to avoid the looser sections of gravel and larger mud puddles. It was only a half mile by gravel road until he reached the paved road into the city. He started to hum a tune that had been in his head most of the morning, he wasn't sure why it was there or where he had heard it. He couldn't remember all of the words, but it went something like "a peace of mind always takes me by surprise, so what would I do without you?"

Paddy admired the brilliant blue of the sky against the yellow gold of the wheat fields; their stubble was poking through the dark earth like an unshaven beard. Lightly touching his own face he realized he had forgotten to shave, and he pictured Madge's smile turning to a frown while she lay in her hospital bed. She probably wouldn't have liked that he was taking his bicycle today either. It had always been good enough to get him to church on Sundays and to the village store to get what they needed. He muttered to himself, "So why would today be any different – it's just a little bit further." He felt a little guilty at the thought of her disdain, but she wasn't there to argue with him. Sadness overtook the guilt.

Lost in thought as he rode, a car startled him from behind, its tires crackling and popping along the gravel road. Paddy wobbled to the side of the road to let the vehicle pass, but it stopped beside him. The electric window of a Chevy half ton rolled down and a man's head poked out of the open window. It was his friend Jim who called out, "Hey Paddy. Where are you headed? Do you need a ride somewhere?"

"No thanks, Jim. I'm just out enjoying the fresh air," Paddy replied, trying to sound cheerful.

"Are you ok, Paddy?" Jim asked.

"Of course, I'm fine." Paddy forced a smile.

"OK see you later then." Jim waved as he drove the Chevy down the road.

Paddy could hear Madge's scolding. "Are you out of your mind, you stubborn old man? You should have accepted a ride!" He answered her aloud, "Maybe."

Wobbling for a distance along the gravel road, Paddy finally reached the paved section of his journey and breathed a sigh of relief. He paused and caught his breath at the stop sign, letting several cars speed by, then struggled to get his bike across the pavement and onto the gravel shoulder of the road. He knew he wasn't making very good time. He needed to pick up the pace. Jim was probably heading to the funeral too and would pass him if he didn't hurry. With grim resolve, he pushed a little harder on the pedals and got the thing moving along at what he thought was a pretty good pace.

As he rode, his mind wandered back to the first time his son Brandon had ridden a bike on his own. They had been practicing in the laneway with Paddy running beside the little blue bicycle holding on to the back of the seat. He had let go, watching the boy with his slightly too long golden hair flipping about in the breeze. He could see the boy wobbling down the laneway, working hard to keep his balance. When he reached the end of the laneway, he just continued pedalling; riding through the gate, bumping up and across the gravel road and right into the long grass and brambles of the ditch on the other side. Paddy had helped him out of the ditch, covered in burrs and scratches, a drop of blood oozing from his bony elbow.

"You did it Brandon!" Paddy had exclaimed. "You were riding!" The boy had beamed with pride. Now tears blurred Paddy's vision as he recalled the pride on Brandon's face as he told his mother the story.

A large transport truck sped by, generating a huge gust of wind in its wake that hit Paddy like a push from behind. He wobbled. His front tire hit a muddy patch of softness which wrenched his handlebars sideways. Paddy was launched through the air into the grass and brambles of the ditch. Lying there stunned for a moment, he mentally checked himself. He wasn't hurt, just wet and his glasses were gone.

"What the heck just hit me?" he thought.

Crawling out of the puddle and pushing himself upright, he spotted his glasses lying in the grass next to him. He picked them up and wiped them on his shirt tail that was sticking out of his jacket. Lifting the bike off the ground, he picked chunks of mud and sod out of the spokes and wheeled it back up the slope towards the highway. If Madge could only see him now...

A raven in the tree above him began to squawk, taunting him, "Awk! Awk! Awk!" it screamed. He yelled back at it. "Just you never mind!"

More determined than ever to be on time, Paddy mounted his muddy bicycle and pushed as hard as he could on the pedals, trying his best to avoid the mud. Lost in his memories he hadn't noticed the dark clouds building on the horizon behind him.

Forty-five minutes of riding brought him into the busy city traffic. Clouds were now blocking the sun and a misty rain had begun to fall, making the city seem gloomy and desperate. Despite the number of cars and people around him, an incredible loneliness filled his soul. His legs were tired. He could only push the pedals slowly - just enough to keep the bike upright. The wet cars were spraying him as they passed, and rivulets of water were running down his glasses making it difficult to see. People were yelling out car windows, "Get off the road!" "Get out of the way!" Cars were zooming by him as he wobbled his way along the space between the parked cars and the rushing traffic. Suddenly something slammed into Paddy's shoulder and he lost control of his bike.

Thump! Paddy's front wheel hit the back of something blue and he was launched forward. The pavement approached his head as if he was in a slow-motion video. He managed to turn his body enough to tuck and roll before he crumbled into the pavement. Winded, he lay there gasping, trying to refill his lungs with air. He could hear Madge's voice egging him on.

"Get up, old man. You're fine. Get on your way or you'll be late."

Paddy opened his eyes. A few people had gathered, staring at him.

They were asking each other, "Is he ok? Did he hit his head?"

The traffic was still streaming by, spraying water everywhere, seemingly oblivious of his dilemma. A little numb and somewhat embarrassed by his soggy state, he slowly pushed himself to sitting while waving off a young woman in a beige raincoat who was bending down to try to help him.

"I'm ok," he said. "I will be fine!"

A boy approached him cautiously. "Are these yours?" he said, holding out Paddy's glasses.

"Oh, thank you, thank you young man." Paddy gently took the glasses and put them on, nodding at the boy. The lad waved and grabbed the hand of the woman in the beige raincoat. They disappeared into the crowd on the sidewalk.

"What are the rest of you staring at?" Paddy grumbled at the people standing around him. "I'm fine! Get on with your own business!"

The people began to dissipate, shrugging and whispering to each other. Paddy rose to his feet, wincing at the pain in his shoulder. He spotted his bike wedged under a blue Toyota and he tugged on the handlebars, sliding it out. The front wheel was bent beyond repair and he wouldn't be riding it any further. Somewhat disoriented, he pulled the bike onto the sidewalk and began to walk, pushing the damaged bike beside him. He wasn't sure which way to go. He stopped a man in a suit holding a newspaper over his head against the rain.

"Could you tell me how to get to the Smith Funeral Home?" Paddy asked.

The man replied, "Yes, it's two blocks down to Jarvis street, then turn right and then it's another block or two on your left. You can't miss the big white sign with the burgundy lettering."

"Thank you!" Paddy replied politely.

He checked his watch and realized he could still be

there on time. Dragging his bike beside him, he limped off in the direction the man had indicated. It didn't take him log to reach Jarvis where there wasn't as much traffic. The Victorian style buildings were set further back from the street, with colourful displays of flowers, carefully trimmed hedges, and immaculate carpet-like lawns. Cars were parked on both sides of the street, and the sidewalk was bordered in huge oak trees that formed a beautiful green archway. The trees appeared to form a shelter but the leaves had collected the rain water and huge drops were splattering down onto Paddy's helmet and clothing. He shivered as the cold water made its way past the collar of his jacket and trickled down his back. Despite the cold and wet, he was relieved that his destination was in sight. Ahead of him was the white sign with burgundy lettering announcing he had reached Smith Funeral Home. He rolled his bike up the long sidewalk towards the porch leading to the huge double doors.

Paddy checked his watch. "Right on time!"

He leaned his battered bicycle against a shrub beside the front stairs, unclipped his helmet, and hung it carefully on the handle bars. Slowly he climbed the stairs, clinging tightly to the painted white handrail. Staggering across the porch, he reached the heavy wooden doors with their ornate iron handles. He tugged. The door opened easily and Paddy was greeted by soft murmuring voices and organ music. He stepped into the warmth of the large foyer. A man in a jet black suit stood in the doorway to the chapel. He could see a few people inside the chapel but he didn't know them. On a table behind the man in the black suit was a framed photograph of a woman. Paddy squinted through his water streaked glasses and hobbled towards it. The heavy door thumped shut behind him and the man in the black suit turned, his sombre expression changing to one of sympathy.

"Mr. O'Brien is that you? You are quite the sight today! Let's get you back into the office so you don't alarm anyone."

Paddy was confused. He was just coming to say goodbye to his beloved wife but the woman in the picture wasn't Madge. Was he in the right place? His knees felt like jelly, and he slowly dropped to the floor, breathing out a huge exhausted sigh. The seat of his pants hit the floor with a squish and muddy water was dripping from his bright orange vest. Paddy vacantly watched the muddy trail make its way along the grain of the golden wood. He wondered where Brandon was. He should be here by now. The funeral was about to start.

"He's here and he doesn't look so good." The man in the black suit was speaking into a cell phone. "Ok I will help him into the office and wait for you there."

The man tucked the cell phone into his jacket and crouched down beside Paddy. He wrapped his arm around Paddy's waist and helped him to his feet.

"Come on Mr. O'Brien. Let's get you into some dry clothes. I have called your son."

"Brandon? Where is he? Why isn't he here already?" Paddy was so confused. Something wasn't right!

The man supported Paddy with one hand and withdrew a huge wad of keys with the other hand. He unlocked the office and pushed open the door, reaching across Paddy to flip on the lights. Paddy made his own way I across the room and sunk into the metal folding chair beside the small but tidy desk. He didn't know how long it was before Brandon rushed into the room.

"Dad, you have to stop doing this! Mr. Purdue has been more than patient!"

Paddy looked into his son's anxious face. Brandon was always a worrier. But why was he dressed so casually in a t-shirt and jeans?

"Let me just go and get cleaned up for your mother's funeral and you should too! The service is at two so we better hurry or it will start without us!"

"Dad, mom's funeral was three weeks ago," Brandon

said gently, putting his arm around Paddy's shoulder. "You've been coming here every time Jim takes a day off and leaves the farm. Mr. Purdue here has been very patient, but you have to stop this!"

"No, it's today. I checked the newspaper clipping on the bulletin board. It's today!"

Tears began to roll down Paddy's dirty unshaven face, leaving streaks in the mud. He didn't know what to do or why this was happening. Brandon's strong arms encircled him, and he was saying to Mr. Purdue, "I'm so sorry about all of this. Go ahead and tend to your work here. I will take care of my dad. This won't happen again."

EMERSON
by Michael Lalonde

Chad annoyed Tyler at times like this. When would he ever learn? Not to accept every spontaneous invite. Not to pay for all of the gas on top of it. And to not—definitely not— be stuck without an exit plan. For here he was, an hour and a half away from Winnipeg in one of those nameless towns that straddle the backbone of the Canada-US boundary.

Tyler yawned and stretched, then sat up in the recliner and scanned the chaos before him. Sleeping bodies. Empty beer cans. Half full glasses of whisky, now makeshift ashtrays. A joint orphaned in a syrupy pool on the coffee table. And the stale smell cigarettes leave the next day.

Near him, Chad asleep on the sofa, wheezed as he exhaled. Tyler wondered how anyone mistook them for twins. Sure their faces looked similar and they shared the same height and dark brown hair. But his hair was shorter than the full mane that sat on Chad's broader shoulders. Chad's neck and arm muscles were thicker; the by-products of farm work. Tyler scratched the stubble on his chin that had appeared overnight. He envied Chad's smoother skin that never needed shaving.

Tyler cursed the clock on the wall. 7:30. Daylight soon and they were supposed to have returned last night. After several shakes he roused Chad from a dead sleep. And when he too realized the time, his buddy swung into action. Chad didn't want to freeze his butt off; he used the remote start-up to bring the Dodge Ram's engine to life.

The two tiptoed over the late sleepers. At the door they donned their coats and gloves and, after sifting through a multitude of footwear, slipped on their boots.

Tyler didn't know or like Chad's friends much. He'd been talked last minute into driving down with him from Winnipeg. Gretna was a town Tyler had never before heard of in his 22 years of living. He'd grown up in Manitoba, thought he knew its every corner. But then he recalled what a teacher had one told him, that the province was the same size as France. He wished it were as warm as France as they stepped out into the freezing darkness.

The crystalline snow crunched beneath them as clouds of steam rose with each breath. They bounded away from the house for the warmth of the truck's cab.

"Crank up the heat, willya," Tyler said, still upset with Chad. He wished Chad had listened last night when he said it was time to leave. But Chad hadn't heard him over the music. Most likely he feigned deafness before disappearing with some girl. It was bad enough Tyler didn't know anyone, but he had nothing in common either. What could they talk about? He didn't like hockey. Didn't care for their juvenile taste in music. And anyway, he didn't live on a farm anymore. Hadn't since his dad pulled up stakes and moved the family back to Winnipeg six years earlier. Tyler used to live on a farm next to the one Chad's family still runs today. Growing up there and having Chad as his best friend were memorable years. But they'd drifted apart and no longer had a common future. Chad stood to inherit the farm; Tyler stood to inherit student debt. At least that is how Tyler chose to see it. Lately he took comfort in reminding himself that he was only one semester from finishing off a degree in Commerce.

After a while the truck pulled out onto the 243 heading east. It occurred to Tyler that Chad had said nothing to him since leaving Gretna.

"Why are you so quiet?" Tyler asked.

"Thinking is all."

"About what?"

Chad let out a long sigh. "My old man will have my hide…" He adjusted the windshield defrost and waited for the glass to clear. "I just remembered that it was my turn to load hay bales for auction this morning." He sped up.

"No rush," Tyler said, annoyed with the ridiculous speed. A crosswind swept snow in front and obscured the way ahead. He worried about black ice, their veering off into the ditch. He worried about the many deer crossing signs racing past them. And then it hit him that that he worried about a lot of things, front and centre being graduation. Once the clock stopped ticking, how would he pay off his student loans? To calm his nerves he thought about the positive. Luckily the way ahead was flat and the road ran straight and in the distance the pink hue of sunrise promised better visibility.

Chad reached under his seat. "You want me to put on a CD?" Tyler wanted him to keep his eye on the road muttered a negative. Chad shrugged. "Okay…talk is what we'll do."

"Yeah. Like we talked last night."

"Can't help it if women find me hot," Chad said, and then laughed when Tyler poked him in the shoulder. "So how about you? You still seeing what's her name?"

"—Krista." Tyler grew quiet, had nothing to say. He couldn't believe how many times he'd reminded Chad about her name. And no matter what he told Chad about Krista—how nice she was, the stuff they had in common, their plans—it always came down to the same question.

"That's it?" Chad asked, glancing back at him. "That's all you've got to say?"

"What's there to share?" Tyler said, his voice sounding exasperated. He wasn't about to tell Chad that Krista planned to study Law at Dalhousie afterwards, that the two of them were seeing less of each other, that it was probably over. "You know that she's from Peterborough. That she's studying in Toronto too—"

"Didya do it?"

"Without fail, you ask that every time."

"Well…didya?"

"None of your business."

Chad dropped one hand from the steering wheel, and glanced sidelong at Tyler. "Guess you didn't," he said, with a wink of an eye. He turned the radio on and tuned in to a station playing the kind of music Tyler decided he longer liked. Nobody but Chad and his friends listened to that crap anymore.

Now it was after sunrise, but the sun hugged the horizon this time of year, and even less light made it through the cover of cloud. Tyler felt more at ease with Chad's driving, for the truck's wide tires and 4X4 transmission ate up the road. Chad's dad had bought the truck new for his twenty-first birthday last year. And even though it was meant as a working truck, Chad didn't owe a nickel on it, or anything else for that matter. Tyler wished the same could be said of him, but going to school in Toronto the past four years had taken its toll on the pocketbook—and it seems—on his heart.

"Now it's my turn to ask?" Chad said. "Why are you so quiet?"

Tyler wished to be left to his own thoughts but spoke just the same. "Been thinking about school. Thinking how it's almost over."

"Suppose you'll be staying in T.O. after this, making the big bucks?"

"Nope."

Chad turned the radio down. "You're not going back to The Peg"

"Probably."

"You're crazy."

Tyler shrugged his shoulders. Chad's obsession with all

of the flash money could buy irked him. He had hoped his friend would dial down the bragging last night. But he didn't. He went on about his banker buddy Tyler, how impressed they were with him at the bank this past summer. How rosy Tyler's future looked. And Tyler despised himself for going along with it, for nothing could be further from the truth. He hated the relentless pressure to meet sales numbers, to treat clients as prey, selling them products and services they didn't need or understand. He wasn't so much hoping to return to Winnipeg. More like he was escaping Toronto.

A sign indicated Highway 75 ahead and to reduce speed.

"So why not T.O.?" Chad asked, not slowing down.

"Too busy, too expensive, too…Toronto."

Chad laughed and shook his head and Tyler supposed he understood (being on the farm and all) that big city living sucked. That returning to Winnipeg might be for the best. More likely it was that Chad did not agree with him. Chad would not admit it, but he would trade places with Tyler in a heartbeat. Chad resented the pressure of taking over the farm; he'd said so, many times in his own way.

"Stop the truck!" Tyler shouted.

"What?"

"I see something." Tyler pointed out to the prairie. "Pull over here…do you see?" Through the blowing snow, something was moving in the field. Cattle, he imagined. They wouldn't last long out here. But with no house or barn in sight, where did they belong?

Chad nudged Tyler's arm and then reached under his side of the seat. "Here." He handed him binoculars. "Have a better look."

"What the hell," Tyler said.

"Whadya see?"

"Somebody's out there. Making their way to the road. But they're falling all over the place." Tyler could not tell if the hooded figure in the parka was a man or a woman.

They remained bent over, taking faltering steps through knee high snowdrifts. "What do we do?"

Tyler shifted the idling truck into drive. "Get the hell out of here is what we do."

"—No wait." Tyler set a firm hand on Chad's forearm. "We can't just leave. Where do you think they're off too?"

"Probably got lost is all. Once they're on this road they'll know where to go. Or maybe someone will come along."

Tyler saw through his friend. Chad had business back on the farm to attend to and nothing was going to get in his way. But he had to give his head a shake if he thought anyone could survive this. Besides, who else would help? They hadn't met anyone else on the road. Wouldn't until Highway 75.

Tyler stared at Chad.

"What?" Chad asked, sounding incensed.

Tyler wondered how his friend could be so clueless at such times. "We have to help."

Chad shook his head. "Okay." He put the truck in park and left it running. "This better be quick."

The two launched themselves into the ditch, trudging through snow, pushing for several minutes against stinging ice crystals stirred up by the wind.

Closer in Tyler glimpsed a beard. The man seemed frozen in the spot, holding his arms close to his chest, one leg up on a mound, the other submerged in snow to the knee, his breath hung in front of him. He wore an unzipped parka and had a blanket-like scarf wrapped several times about his neck. When the wind flipped back his hood he made no attempt to right it. Tyler considered calling out to keep him walking their way, but he knew the wind would drown him out.

The man tried to push them away at first, then stumbled to his knees. They gripped each of them an arm and wrapped it about their shoulders to support his weight. And as they struggled forward the man had trouble

154

taking steps. Several times his knees gave way, and he was dead weight, prompting them to prop him up each time before continuing. Tyler half-wondered if they'd make it back to the truck, and when they arrived, they eased him into the middle seat.

Tyler wasted no time removing the shivering man's wet coat, flimsy gloves and boots. He studied his dark skin. Probably he'd crossed in the middle of the night.

Chad said, "It's one of them."

"Yes. It's one of them."

"So…we won't be driving him home."

"I know."

Tyler shook the snow from the man's boots and set them under the heat vent, and then he felt the man's neck. He had a weak pulse. His breathing was shallow and he slipped in and out of consciousness.

From behind the seat Chad fished for a blanket, Tyler supposed, kept for just such occurrences. More likely he believed he'd use it for the comfort of his female companions. Tyler wrapped their patient in the blanket trying to recall further what he had learned in wilderness survival class back in high school. That this was a case of hypothermia he needed no convincing. He wished they could offer him a warm drink—hot chocolate, coffee, tea even—for it was crucial to keep the core warm.

Exhausted, they sat in silence, Tyler wondering when— not if—Chad would bail. Of course he had to get his butt back to the farm. But first things first.

"We've got to find help," Tyler said over the half-conscious man sitting between them. Thinking Chad had not listened the first time, he began, "I said, we've—"

"I heard you."

"What do you suggest, then?"

"If I have to drive out of my way, losing time and all, then I need to make it worth my while."

"You want him to pay you to take him to a hospital?"

"Think about it," Chad said. Tyler noticed him looking

155

back out onto the field. "They come expecting handouts."

"Shhh. He's right here."

"I don't care," Chad said, his voice rising. "He's sleeping and in any case he probably doesn't understand what we're saying." Then he lowered his voice. "All's I'm saying is that they shouldn't expect a free ride the moment they arrive, especially when they're breaking the law."

Tyler threw his hands up in frustration. "Okay, then. Let's just go and we'll figure something out along the way."

In minutes Highway 75—the way back to Winnipeg—was upon them. Chad signalled his intentions to take it.

"No, no, no," Tyler said. "Keep going to Emerson. That's where they're taking them." He felt on thin ice now, thinking Chad's patience was just about spent. "I know it's out of your way, but it'll be the quickest."

When they pulled up to a community centre a short while later, their passenger stirred. He stammered, "C-C-Canada?" Tyler nodded and smiled. "I want live in Canada," the man added in halting English. Then he tapped his chest with his fingers. "Abdul."

Tyler was grateful to see the feeling had returned to the man's fingers. He looked up at Chad who turned away to view the street.

Tyler went inside to make inquiries. He came out minutes later with a burly man dressed in a fireman's uniform.

"I'm going to stay with him," Tyler said to Chad, taking a hold of Abdul.

"Florence F'ing Nightingale." Chad laughed. "He's just a refugee."

"We're all refugees," Tyler said

"Whatever."

Tyler and the others watched Chad's truck disappear, and then he turned to Abdul.

"Your new home," he said

"Yes," Abdul smiled. "My new home, inshallah."

CLUE ON A COFFEE CUP
by R.O.

It's Christmas eve, 1999 in Vancouver B. C. Brian has been digging around in his girlfriend Samantha's walk in pantry for five minutes now and still can't find the sugar, that she was so certain was in there, and Brian, always trying to be the nice and helpful man, offered to fetch it for her.

"Honey, I can't find it anywhere." Brian called out.

"Do you want me to help?" Samantha calls out, "I really need it, I promised my mom that we would make the cranberry sauce this year, and we're heading out there tomorrow." Brian hears his best friend Jason's voice in the background.

"Don't worry Sam, I'll help him out."

"You sure Jason?" she replies

"Yeah, we ran out of wine anyways." He says

"Okay, well if you need me just-"

"We'll be fine." Jason reassures her.

The pantry door opens then and he closes it behind him.

"Hey man, wow, I thought she'd never let me come in."

"Don't take it personally, that's just her." Brian says as he continues looking through the boxes on the shelves, he feels Jason's sweater brush against his arm as leans back

157

against the shelf beside him. He watches from the corner of his eye as Jason puts a cigarette between his lips and lights it.

"Jeez, Jason! You can't do that in here." Brian stops and turns towards him offering him a glare.

"Oh, I'm sorry. I didn't know this was some rule." Jason teases as he lifts up his hands in a mock peace gesture with the cigarette and lighter still clutched in one hand.

"It's not a rule, it's just, you know etiquette. Not that you would understand the meaning of the word." Brian turns back towards the pantry shelf.

"You want one?" Jason asks as he blows out a large puff of smoke.

"What the hell, sure." Brian takes the pack and lighter and lights one up for himself. He takes a long drag and grins back at Jason.

"You are such a bad influence on me." He says.

"I know." Jason replies as he turns towards the other wall and begins to rummage through the shelves.

"So what are we looking for again?" He asks Brian.

"Sugar and I think you wanted wine." He replies.

"Ah yes." Jason murmurs, grabbing a bottle of red wine and the corkscrew beside it from the top shelve. Brian watches him as he removes the cork and takes a swig of the wine straight form the bottle.

"Ah, refreshing." Jason sighs. "Well, would you look what we have here?" He grabs the box of sugar that had been hidden behind the wine.

"Thanks man, your my saviour." Brian say's reaching for it.

Suddenly, Jason's face changes then, his dark brown eyes glint a different shine. He holds the box farther away from him.

"You want it? Come get it."

Brian reaches for it again, "Come on man, just give it to me."

"You want it?" Jason says, "Then come over here." The dim lighting of the pantry plays off his blonde shaggy hair that falls in his face.

"Fine." Brian says, annoyed. He walks over to him and takes hold of the box.

"Here's your sugar, sugar." Jason whispers as he leans in and kisses him.

Brian pushes back in a panic. He feels like his hear is going to beat out of his chest.

"Jason, what are you doing? No!" He looks back at Jason and sees a pained look in his eyes.

"I'm sorry, uh, just forget about it. Forget about all of it." He opens the door then, heading out.

Samantha stares back at him.

"We found the sugar, here's the wine." Jason basically throws both items at her.

"Thanks Jason, hey, is everything okay?" She asks.

"Yeah, I'm just tired, I think I'm going to head on home." Brian steps out of the pantry and watches as he snatches his coat and rushes out the apartment door.

"What happened in there?" Samantha asks.

"Nothing Brian answers touching her arm. "You want me to help you with that cranberry sauce?"

Present Day

Brian feels the tears rolling down his cheeks as he woke. The memory always ends the same way, the wrong way. Even in his dream's Brian can't change the ending. He can't change anything.

Brian should have kissed him back, followed him out of the apartment. Perhaps then everything could have been different, none of this would have ever happened.

Even though he tries not to, Brian can't help but replay the last conversation he had with Jason five months ago at the restaurant he was always adamant in going to, before Jason completely vanished off the face of the earth.

"Brian, do you ever think about that Christmas Eve at

159

Samantha's?" Jason had asked. Brian was looking out the window at that moment but turned his head back to face him. He did, all the time. Did he think of him the same? He stared into Jason's eyes, even after all these years, he was still as beautiful as he was when they were that much younger, maybe even more so. Before he had a moment to respond, Jason started up again.

"I don't know why I said that. I mean, we were just kids right? Let's change the subject, shall we?" He seemed so distracted, far away. Brian knew something was wrong, but just then his phone vibrated on the table beside him.

"You should take it." Jason said, nibbling at his cuticles.

"No, hey, is everything okay with you?" Brian asked, wanting to get to the bottom of it.

"Yeah, you should take it. I'll see you later."

"Okay, please text me alright?" Brian said watching him get up from his seat and walk away. He can still see his black suit, his now long blond hair tied into a ponytail. He watched with concern as Jason tapped the tips of his slender fingers on the side of his thighs as he made his way to the exit. He should have probed him further, made him talk. But he didn't.

Now it felt like it was too late. Not that Brian ever let that hinder his search for him.

"Where the heck, are you, huh?" He murmured as he looked at the photo of them together on the nightstand. It was taken the night they met, at the college tavern. Brian remembered it vividly.

It was 1997; the snow was coming down heavy, covering everything in a thick, white blanket. Brian was just leaving the bar when he seen a young man wearing nothing but a flannel shirt, band tee, and ripped up jeans wandering around the parking lot.

"Hey, do you need some help?" Brian called out, walking towards the stranger.

"Yeah, I can't find my car." He could smell the beer on

his breath. He would drive him home.

"Well, maybe you could show me what it looks like, and I could drive you home. I'm a DD, you know, designated driver?" He stuffed his fists deep into the pockets of his black pea coat.

"Why doesn't that surprise me?" The man said. Brian looked down at himself then, he was wearing a black dress coat, slacks, and black patent loafers. The difference was uncanny. He looked like the cool guy at the party, while Brian appeared as a yuppie know-it-all, who never got in trouble for anything.

"Awe, why not. I need some help anyways. Names Jason Mellor by the way." He casually gave Brian his hand and he shook it.

"Brian, Brian Eastern." And that was how it all started. For several minutes, they wandered around that parking lot, talking about everything and anything. Brian never shared so much in his life.

After a while, both of them fell silent.

"Man, I'm drunk." Jason finally broke out.

"Yeah, even I could have told you that." Brian said nudging him in the arm.

"No, I mean really drunk. Dude, we've been walking around for over twenty minutes, and I don't even own a stupid car."

"What? You mean to tell me I've been freezing my butt off all this time, and you don't even own a car?" Brian was ready to lose it on this guy.

"Hey bro, I'm sorry alright? You know, besides, you're not as much of a jerk as I thought. Wanna go back inside?" He threw his hands up, a peace offering.

"Yeah, okay. Let's go inside." Brian and Jason headed back to the bar and talked all night, just like they would for many other nights, even years.

Brian took all those times for granted, he knew he did. He forces himself to get up and make his way to the shower. So much has changed since then; Brian was now an elite lawyer, a partner of his own firm in the city. Jason completed an art degree and transitioned into a well-off real estate agent, that was, until he quit, which Brian discovered after calling his office when he didn't hear back from him.

There were still so many missing pieces to the puzzle; Brian thought as he turned on the shower head and felt the beads of water strike his face. Their stories kept playing in his head like a film, over and over again. But it doesn't bring him back. It doesn't give him any more answers. It's all just empty, hollow.

He carefully steps out of the shower and stands in front of his mirror, staring back at his own reflection. He is far from the young man he once was. His black hair cropped shorter, his features more chiselled, his blue eyes paler now, more knowing.

Jason used to always tell him after he broke off his engagement with Samantha, that he could literally have any woman that he wanted, that Samantha was boring. The truth is that it had nothing to do about whether or not Samantha was boring, and everything to do with how he really felt about Jason Brian wanted him. When she eventually cheated, it finally made him feel he never needed to pretend anymore, slightly.

In Brian's soul, he was open. To the rest of society though, he was not. As far as they knew, he was the average heterosexual single man.

But sooner than later, he knew, women will discover the real reason why he always declines their offers of affection.

He did try dating a couple of times, and although they both put the effort in, he was never capable of recreating the feelings he had for Jason.

Brian brushed his teeth and looked up again into the mirror. He looked tired. He needed coffee. He needed many things.

Brian padded back into the bedroom and grabbed one

of the several designer suits hanging in his closet, and put it on. He looked like a different man, a new man. A man, who was self- assured, knew where he was headed in life. In most ways, it was the truth.

Jason would know what words to say to him to snap Brian out of this. But, alas, Jason isn't here, is he?

He came out of his bedroom, grabbed his coat, and headed out the door.

For the first time all morning, Brian was able to find some of the solace he needed in the large crowded streets. Here he blended with the other's wandering to and from their buy lives. He didn't have to think of anything really, just moving his feet.

He is already aware that he will follow his typical morning routine of going to the neighbourhood coffee shop 'Little Beans', to get his morning fix. He owns a coffee maker that Samantha had bought him several years before, but Brian was always too lazy to up and make a pot for himself.

As Brian enters through the glass doors, he is taken aback by how many other people are there doing exactly the same as him. There must be about fifteen other people lined up. A young man standing in front of him is wearing an awful neon yellow, blue, and white wind breaker and lime green high top shoes and is talking to his friend beside him that looks equally as vibrant.

"Seriously, you should hear the guitar riff. I think they might play at this weekend's festival."

"Nice!" The friend says "Are you gonna go?"

"Totally, you should come too, eh?" They lay five each other, and Brian could remember those days when he was young.

Suddenly the doors open behind him and a woman and her young daughter and preteen son step inside.

"Mommy, can I have one of those powdered doughnuts?" The daughter asks.

"How about an old fashioned one?"

"Okay." The young girl says

"Kevin?" The mother says to her son.

"Kevin! Can you take those things out of your ears for even a moment?" She says more direct.

"What?" The son answers her, clearly annoyed.

"Do you want anything?"

"Yeah, an espresso, two shots."

"You want an espresso?" The mother says, stunned. "You're thirteen for goodness sake! Where did you have an espresso?"

"Chris's mom makes them for us all the time."

"Well, I guess I will have to make a call to his mother than. Is bottled water okay?"

"Sure." The son mutters.

A phone rings, presumably hers.

"Hello? Hi honey, Uh-huh. No, I can't really hear you; I'm at the coffee shop with the kids. What? You have to work late again? But, what about our dinner plans? Okay, I'll just order Chinese. Yep, love you too, bye."

"Mommy, I need to pee." The girl whispers to her mother.

"Okay, mommy's paying; your brother will take you. Kevin, can you take your sister to the bathroom please?"

Brian finally reaches the counter to face a barista.

"What can I get for you this morning sir?"

It always makes Brian flinch when he hears someone call him by that title. It never ceases in making him feel old.

"I'll have a small coffee, black, with cinnamon." He asks.

"What the heck is wrong with you?" Jason would say when they got coffee together. "Why coffee and cinnamon? That's just weird man, you're doing it wrong."

Truth is, Brian always drank his coffee that way. It was the same way as his mother took it. He considered it his form of remembering her since she died eight years ago.

"That'll be coming right up. Can I have your name?

164

Sorry, we don't typically ask, it just busier than usual today." He says as he turns his thumb towards a young woman with a thick braided rope of black hair going down her back. He heard her curse as she spilt coffee on herself.

"We even had to ask our stacker to help this morning."

"That's not a problem. It's Eastern." He says watching the boy jot it down quickly onto a small notepad. He handed it to the stacker, as she turns so her eyes meet Brian's, for some reason it makes him unusually nervous, he feels himself sweat slightly.

"No kidding." The mother chimes in from behind Brian. "You wouldn't happen to be the lawyer Brian Eastern from Eastern and Lowe, would you?"

He watches for a moment as the stacker pours his order into a cup that is placed away from the others. He adjusts his tie as he turns to face the woman behind him, placing on his professional mask, and giving her the smile that he has become well known for. She's wearing an oversized hoodie and jeans; her hair is placed in a messy bun. Her face is covered in several laugh lines. She seems kind, calm.

"Yes, ma'am, that would be me." Brian says

"Gosh, well you're even more handsome in person!" The woman gushes. "I saw you in the paper the other day, you just won that massive case, didn't you? I'm Maria by the way." She offers him her hand and he shakes it.

"Yes, we did. We are all quite pleased with the outcome. It was a pleasure to meet you Maria."

"It was nice meeting you as well." The woman says as the barista watches impatiently as Brian leaves to wait for his order.

"Sorry, yes, I'll have a small black coffee, an old fashioned and a bottled water." The woman says as her children come scampering over to her.

Brian watches on as the stacker places his order on the counter. After a brief moment, it appears that the barista and stacker are now arguing over something, she takes off her green smock she is wearing, and hands it to him with a shrug, before going into the backroom.

"Eastern, Callahan, your orders are ready!" The barista shouts out. Brian and the mother head over to the counter, he hadn't even seen her standing beside him. The woman reaches for her order first and takes a sniff.

"Uh, that smells like cinnamon. Oh gross!" She say's shaking her head.

"I think you grabbed mine by mistake." Brian say's reaching for it.

"Yeah, I think I did." She says, passing it back to him. "Hey! Watch it!" She says as the stacker from before dodges between them. She is wearing a violet scarf that drapes over one shoulder of her brown leather jacket.

"Sorry." She mutters as she glances up at Brian before leaving out the door. He watches her head down the street through the glass windows.

Why is she so important? Why was she staring at me? Brian wonders as he leaves the coffee shop. He sees his bus waiting at the bus stop at the corner and he rushes to catch it.

What eventually makes him twitch though is what he finds when he enters inside.

At the front, in the first row of seats is no other than the stacker girl from the coffee shop. Brian feels something in him go cold as she stares up at him with her wide, green eyes. Was she following him? He anxiously looks around for a seat, any seat that is far away from her. But of course, the only available spot is the one behind her. Cautiously, and with a sense of unease, he sits down and watches as she takes the elastic out of her hand, unfurling the braid and letting her hair fall in dark, wavy tendrils down her back. She seemed like the type of woman that most men would find attractive, but Brian was not most men.

She never turns to look back at him, which Brian takes as a good sign. He allows himself to relax ever so slightly, and takes a sip of his coffee, letting the warm liquid go down his throat as he lowers his eyes.

That is when everything stops, the word around him freezes while Brian is left spinning out of control. On the cup is a scrawl of handwriting, of which Brian now knew by heart. It was Jason's.

He hears his heart pounding in his ears as he carefully reads every line:

Brian – I know you've been looking for me. If you want to know where I am, follow her. – Jason

He lets the coffee cup fall form his hand onto the floor of the bus, letting the warm liquid pool everywhere. He was supposed to work today, but this call's for that much needed time off. They could more than make do without him for one day. He watches as the woman turns her attention on the spilt coffee, then back at him before pulling down the metal lever to stop the bus. Brian feels as if his legs can't move fast enough as he gets up from the seat and follows her out the Plexiglas doors and back out on the sidewalk.

Brian is able to stay steadfast on her trail as they move down the street. A few passersby weave in and out between them, but he never takes his eyes off her.

After a while, she turns and starts walking down the main sidewalk, as Brian follows close behind. It is in that moment that for the first time he considers if he actually wants to know what could have happened to Jason, but he has come too far to stop now. Brian waits for her to signal to him before moving closer she stops walking and sits on a sidewalk bench, before she waves him over to sit down beside her.

She speaks first. "Hello Brian, before you go and ask me a hundred thousand questions like Jason said you would, he wanted you to know that he is safe and perfectly fine." Brian catches his breath.

"Who are you? Where is he? When can I see him?" He rambles on.

"Woah, hold your horses, okay? You look like you're going to have a stroke."

"You have no idea what I've been through." He says.

"No, you're right. I don't. But Jason did tell me how close you two were." She reaches for something out of her pocket, and pulls out a folded white envelope, which she hands to him.

"Here, Jason wanted me to give this to you as soon as I had the opportunity. I have no idea what it says really, it's just for you."

Brian took it in his hands and stared at it for a long moment before ripping it open. The woman kicked at a stone with the tip of her boot.

He felt tears welling in his eyes as he pulled out the letter, it wasn't much, but it was at least something that would answer the questions that had been rolling around in his mind for months, the type of answers that had the potential to change his life.

Brian- it read;

If you're reading this, I guess I'm free to say that you got my message that I had written on that little coffee cup, and followed Melissa. Yes, that's her name, she is a cousin of mine, and you two never met before.

The first thing you need to know is that my old office passed on the message that you called, and I love you, and I can't begin to tell you how sorry I am, for all of this. The second thing you need to know is that I desperately want to see you again, and make things right between us."

The last time we met, I could tell that you knew something was wrong, and there was. I should have told you Brian, I know, but I just didn't know where to start.

About four months before I left, I had made several poor property investments, and I came close to losing the shirt off my back.. This I could have handled, but of course there was more. My father had passed. He was always a healthy man, or so I thought. Truth is he was suffering from heart disease, but never said a word. I guess when the going gets tough; I'm stubborn like my old man. The last time I seen him nearly a year before, he was working in his home shop, still fixing cars even though he had long retired from doing it full time. He tried to make small talk with me, say how proud he was of what I was doing, but I know he always resented me leaving him for the city; he wanted me to run the shop after him. I sometimes wonder if I should've stayed, especially now.

The embarrassment of the financial struggles and the pain of loss were too much for me to bear, never really being able to talk openly about these things, always being the one to fix things, rather than talk about it, I thought the only solution was for me to leave.

So I gave my notice to the office, called Melissa, who I had run into at dad's funeral, and she agreed to let me live with her in Saskatoon until I could figure myself out. I nearly left everything behind, but some things I could never let go.

I had always planned on coming back to you, Brian, truth is, when I mentioned that Christmas eve from all those years ago, it was my attempt to make you change my mind. I love you, I always have. But I could never shake the fear that you didn't feel the same way, and when you didn't say anything when I breached the subject, I thought my assumptions were correct. I'm hoping I was dead wrong.

A few weeks ago, I checked properties on a whim, something I promised myself I would never do again, but something nagged at me that I should. As I searched, fate had found a way to call out to me. There was a property I seen that appeared vaguely familiar, after a moment I realised that it was where we met for the first time. It was more than mere chance, it was destiny. The owner was selling it for a low price, which I could afford. So I called, bought it, packed my bags and headed back to you.

Melissa, looking for a new start chose to come with me. In what turned out to be a pleasant coincidence, the job she received was one of which happened to be at the coffee shop that you went to everyday. The one thing I didn't know about you. Melissa told me this after she seen you come in, recognizing you from the photos I shared. I was happy, but I still didn't yet know how to face you.

One morning, Melissa left her shift and found you standing on the street you didn't see her, you were looking up to the sky, she then heard you whisper my name. In that moment I thought maybe we had a chance.

I couldn't hide from you any longer so I created this whole scenario to show you that you needn't search anymore, I was here, and I was yours.

As you're reading this, I am sitting in Woodridge Park, on a green bench overlooking a large maple tree waiting for you. I may not be able to bring us the past we deserved back then, but I can give you our future.

Love, Jason.

Brian stayed silent for a long while, letting the tears fall freely. He would have been there for Jason, he would be there now. He wished he had of said before what he felt to him. Brian would be damned if he left anything unsaid ever again.

He stuffed the letter back into his pocket and looked up at Melissa.

"I'd really like to see him now."

When they finally reached the park, it was Melissa who found him, sitting on the bench watching the leaves fall of the large maple tree. His hair was short, and slightly grown out like it had once been before, he looked beautiful.

"That's him." She said, touching Brian's shoulder.

"I know, I don't know how--" He started before she interjected.

"I'm just happy I could help." She said, "You need to go to him, I think you both have waited long enough.

Brian started to head towards the bench, when he turned back to look at Melissa who smiled and waved, Brian waved back at her before heading off.

Carefully, he took his seat beside Jason, who turned to face him, tears welling in his eyes. Brian reached up and brushed one off his cheek with his thumb.

"I don't know where to start." Jason whispered

"I do." Brian said as he took his face in his hands and gave him a light kiss.

When it was over, the two of them sat together for a long while, the first snowfall of the year had begun. Brian reached out his hand, and caught several snowflakes in his palm. He realised the winter was and always will be what brings him and Jason together. It was the heart coming home.

A MAP OF THE MOON
by Marion Agnew

Standing on the deck as the early evening sun drops behind me toward the horizon, I can't help but sing.

"Tonight, tonight." I la-la a few more measures. Tonight, on this warm July evening, Ricky Johnson—Rick, I should call him; we're adults now—is coming over. Twenty-ish years ago, in our Grade 12 production of West Side Story, Rick was in the back row of Shark dancers. I was an unnamed Jet girlfriend. I tried out only because he dared me, as he challenged me in physics and French, as I challenged him in chemistry and history and Latin.

Inside on the kitchen counter, my cell buzzes. I ignore it, as I have for the two weeks since my father's death. I think yet again about turning it off, but that feels too final. For "tonight, tonight," I prefer limbo.

I sing "won't be just any night" and shiver. I've spent those two weeks imagining just how tonight will go. Ricky will stand here, on my parents' deck, holding a glass of wine—no, Scotch; Scotch is better for him, though I'll have wine—against the slight paunch under his plaid shirt. His snapping blue eyes will be puffy; his wavy brown hair a little too long and streaked with grey. He'll speak of his life, charming as always, and lean in to me as I say…something I can't quite imagine. But it'll be the right thing, the perfect thing, the thing that shows him how whole and fabulous I am without him. And—this is the most important part—it'll spark his regret. He'll recognize that everything his life has lacked stands right here, right next to him.

And now that I have another chance in my life for course correction, even though my life, admittedly, has been mostly course correction, I will take advantage of that moment to seize my future with both hands.

And I'll say it: "Drop dead, Rick."

Only I won't say it that way, not exactly. Too cavalier, this soon after Daddy's death.

Something rings inside the house—though I hope it's the doorbell and Ricky, it's the house phone. I press my ear to the screen door to listen while my parents' answering machine picks up.

Roger, my whatever-he-is, technically my husband but maybe not for much longer, has the grace to leave a message.

"Beth. Hi. I've been trying your cell, but…um. Just calling to check in? Wondering what's going on, I guess. How you are." A pause. "We should probably talk, right?" His voice is tired. "Okay. Please call." A click.

"Okay," I say to the dim room. I'll call. Not tonight, though.

Tonight. I try to sing again, but it's hard to banish Roger. He's the perfect example of how relationships are like sharks. At least I think it's sharks—whatever it is that has to keep moving so it can breathe. If it doesn't move, it dies. Roger and I stopped moving long ago. I'm just not one hundred percent sure we're dead.

Back at the railing, I watch the eastern sky take on colour as the sun, on the other side of the house, slants ever closer to the horizon. Even after the sun goes behind the trees, the twilight will linger. Ricky and I will stand right here and watch the moon rise.

Just two weeks earlier, my father and I sat up all night in his bedroom, side by side, breathing together. A cannula

174

beneath his nose fed oxygen into his nostrils. We watched the night fade into a grey dawn through the bay window in the bedroom overlooking the lake.

Storm clouds had gathered and blotted out the still-waxing moon. Then the wind came up and whipped the lake into swells. Our shoreline, protected from most storms, soon caught real waves, iced with curling froth.

"Awfully fierce for this late in June," my father said softly. During the past few hours, his laboured breathing had calmed. Just signing papers to receive hospice care had helped him relax.

"Even with the clouds, you can see the sky getting lighter." I sat folded into a small club chair next to his recliner, an afghan on my knees. Long ago—what felt like days but was probably only hours—I had reached for his hand where it lay on his blankets. Now I held it out of habit. Together, we watched the wide, shallow bay. Waves broke along the beach, long rollers. The picture was twelve hours out of place, a late afternoon lake in the early morning.

"It would be sunrise about now, wouldn't it?" He looked at his wrist, forgetting again he'd given me his watch a few days ago, when his arms swelled purple. I'd taken his plain gold wedding band at the same time. Mom had died ten years before, but he still wore the ring. To keep the widows away, he said.

"Past. It's nearly 6, and the sun peeks up just after 5 these days." I had read this to him from the newspaper, weather reports and daily averages and highs and lows, anything to help distract him from his difficulty breathing. But I always forgot to look at sunrises and sunsets as they happened outside in the world. My mind was full of my father—his ports and thrush and IV drips and oxygen.

"Look!" He motioned with his chin. "Geese!"

Four adults and six growing goslings glided into the surf in a lull between sets of rolling waves. Most stayed near shore, but a couple ventured a few meters out. They seemed hungry. I wondered when I'd eaten last. I wondered if Dad would eat again.

"Your mother loved this view. That last year, she'd sit here for hours, watching the ravens do acrobatics, looking for deer in the yard." His voice gentle, he sighed past other memories, the ones he'd spoken of non-stop for six months.

How Mom made a cake on what would have been the first birthday of the baby that died two years before my older sister Marilyn was born, a chocolate cake with chocolate frosting, and Mom cut him a wedge in the kitchen and served it to him without saying anything, not one word. He wondered why she'd baked this cake in the middle of the week, but he'd let it go, grateful for something sweet, and it wasn't till she was crying at bedtime that he'd remembered.

How they'd saved up from teaching, and his nights and weekend shifts at the hockey rink, to buy this house on the lake, thirty years ago when nobody lived out here and land was cheap and the roads weren't paved, sometimes not even plowed in the winter. How happy they'd been to raise Marilyn and me out here, even happier after retiring early, till Mom found the lump.

How he had tried but ultimately failed to deal with Mom's clothing and keepsakes after she died. The sight of her hairbrush on the dresser had given him both pain and comfort, until the pain had faded and he could cling to the comfort.

He'd said, "Sorry to leave the whole house to you and Marilyn to deal with, kiddo." I'd waved it away, pretending he still had months or years left in which he'd help us.

I knew better, though. He lay in Mom's recliner, his cannula attached to a tube that snaked to the large oxygen concentrator in the corner of the room. I stared at the tube, thinking about serpents and Eve and wisdom and all I'd learned about oxygen and saturation levels and valves and flow rates. And the stubbornness, the courage it takes,

176

sometimes, just to keep breathing.

"He's brave." Dad pointed out at the geese. The largest one stood on a rock with his back to the lake, watching the shoreline and his flock feeding in the shallows. As we watched, a wave came up behind the gander and lifted him onto its crest, surfing him the ten meters into shore. Once he found his feet under him again, he turned to face the lake and flapped his raised wings, honking.

We laughed. My father said, "That's right, my friend. Don't take any crap from Mother Nature. You show those waves who's boss."

Suddenly I blinked back tears. I whispered to our clasped hands, "That's you, Daddy."

He chuckled. "Not any more. I fought a good fight, but…no." His voice cracked, and I looked up. His lower lip trembled. "That's you, now, Bethy."

Then I put my head down on his blanketed lap and sobbed. He took his hand from mine and laid it on my head. We said many things to each other during his illness. But that's what I remember.

He died the next morning, a bright Sunday morning late in June.

Word got around in the mysterious way it does. Starting at noon, casseroles and salads and deli trays appeared in waves as people gave a brief courtesy knock and then bustled into the kitchen, sometimes patting my shoulder on their way in or out. Mid-afternoon, Marilyn arrived and after our brief cry together, I officially went off duty.

Marilyn had ordered me to rest. But first, I moved clothing into my parents' bedroom. With aunts and cousins—though not Roger—coming for the funeral, we'd need all the bedroom space. I had spent so much time in my parents' room that I was sick of it, but I couldn't bear the thought of someone else sleeping there.

I lay on the bed staring up at the ceiling, hating anyone who was alive and talking about my father over cold cuts and potato salad.

When I couldn't look at the ceiling anymore, I flipped through the science magazines I'd read to my father as he lay in his chair.

Finally Marilyn stuck her head in, voice tight. "I know you're tired, but could you please come make some rounds?"

I groaned and fell back on the bed. "I don't know what to say," I told the ceiling. "I don't care about anything right now."

"Just make some small talk."

"But all I can think about is Daddy and our magazines." I sat up. "He'd have loved this. It's a tardigrade. A bug, sorta, that lives in outer space." I held up the open magazine to show her the picture. "Or, I don't know, not a bug. An animal. A worm? Like sea monkeys, those brine shrimp. They go dormant in dry environments and then wake up when there's water around."

"Okay, but could you at least come say 'thank you' to people who loved our parents?" Beneath Marilyn's sadness, I saw her "older sister" face: a mixture of amusement and annoyance.

"Sorry," I said to the magazine lying open in my lap.

She shook her head. "It's okay. I know you've been working hard." She sighed. "What I really dread is this house. We'll have to deal with it soon—this summer. It's … overwhelming."

I looked up. "One step at a time, right?"

"Sure. Look, take a shower and come out here. You'll feel better."

I knew she was right. After a shower, clean clothes, and ten minutes of psyching myself up, I emerged. I spoke to a few people, put some food on a paper plate, and leaned against a counter in the kitchen with several of my parents' friends.

A few nods in my direction were followed by murmurs

of "So sorry." Then Mrs. Ranta filled me in. "I was mentioning Mrs. Johnson. Marguerite. You know her? Son about your age."

Mrs. Johnson, as in Ricky? I swallowed potato salad and nodded.

"Well, she's not good. The son, he's here to stay with them for a few weeks so the sister can have a break."

"I'm so sorry she's sick," I said, trying to keep my voice casual. "This son, this is Ricky—Richard, right? Do you know exactly what he does?"

Shrugs all around the kitchen.

"Something at Queen's Park, too fancy for me to understand," said Mr. Gordon. "Never married, did he?"

My breath caught, and that was when my vision of the middle-aged plaid-shirted Ricky Johnson appeared, two decades overlaid on the Ricky Johnson whose every opinion I once knew far better than my own, who had felt like someone I'd be with forever. But, as it had turned out, someone I hadn't thought of once since Daddy got sick, and, hand to God, not for many years before that.

"Oh yes, I think so. Years ago now," said Mrs. Ranta with a shrug. "It didn't last long. Not like marriages in our day."

Immediately I had no room in my head for Ricky or anyone else. All I could hear were my father's marriage stories—their baby and sacrifices, the lump and his pain, and at last his comfort alone. I missed him all over again, like a knife to my lungs, and I wanted nothing to do with anyone else and their gossip.

I managed to flash a smile around the kitchen before slipping back into the bedroom with a couple of chocolate chip cookies. I tried and failed to read more about tardigrades. Eventually, I lay back again, staring at the ceiling.

"Bethy," my father said. I knew he wasn't there, but I heard him anyway. "Bethy, don't you say life's unfair. Don't you even start with that 'woe is me' crap. You made your choices, fair and square. You're the one who eloped with that American and moved to Ohio. Ohio, for Chrissake."

He said it the way he always did, like Roger didn't have a name, just a nationality; like Ohio was the end of the earth, not a place with cities and jobs, where people might choose to get married and live on purpose. Until they chose not to. Like I had. Maybe.

And that life in Ohio, with Roger, had been useful. I'd learned to handle the public and telephones, and that helped during Daddy's illness. The personal care workers, his oncologist, even the pastor at Mom's United Church who stopped by occasionally. It had surprised me when he offered communion, and I was shocked when Daddy accepted.

"For your mother," he said quietly to me as the minister readied his cracker and vial of juice. And for the billionth time, I had blinked back tears.

So in part thanks to Roger, those six months with my father had been found time, numinous, and I'd been somehow right—right skills, right place, right time, right me. But now I had to start my regular life again, with its maybe-endings and snapped tempers and the decisions I'd postponed by drinking wine and waiting for Ricky to come over.

When the doorbell actually does ring, my vision of Middle-Aged Ricky is nowhere in sight. Instead, a young-looking hardbody in a tight black t-shirt throws himself at me and grabs me in a bear hug.

"Elizabeth! Oh, Beth, how good to see you!"

The next thing I know, I'm sitting behind him on a motorcycle, wearing his helmet. Its weight makes my neck wobble and pulls me wildly off-balance.

I think he says something about going down the road to the park, but his voice is muffled, and I say, "You're not legal!" because of the helmet law, but then he starts the engine and I grab his waist and it's lean under my hands. I press into his back, and the world is loud and throbs beneath me. The speed threatens to take off the top of my head. All my previous plans have scattered like confetti.

Then we're back and more or less in my fantasy. The more part is that we're standing on the deck, watching the fingernail-sliver moon rise as the dusk grows around us. The less part is pretty much everything else, including the talking, which isn't easy. He's refused wine, so I nurse my glass.

I've asked after his mother and expressed concern for her illness. His responses have been monosyllables, and he didn't, in turn, say or ask anything about Daddy. To cover my hurt, I offer at random, "So what do you do, anyway?"

"Hah. Seriously, you haven't stalked me on Facebook?"

"Sorry, I've been busy." I bite back the rest of that sentence, "caring for my father, you know, who died recently?" and make my voice casual. "Ohio's in a whole different country, you know."

He smiled. "I guess." After a pause, he asks, "So…how long has it been, anyway?"

I gulp some wine. Then I look at the moon.

One warm June day near the end of Grade 13, Ricky and I cut our late-morning class and went to up to The Bluffs to sit on the rocks. We could see the shallow bowl of Boulevard Lake, and farther beyond, Lake Superior. Closer to us, the nubile world flourished in the sunshine of the lengthening days.

The mixed stand of evergreens thrust out new lime-green growth, shocking against their darker needles.

"Look," Ricky had said. "The red pines are all teenaged boys, giving the world the finger. But the balsams are like girls, showing their new manicures." As I laughed, he spread his fingers and affected a falsetto. "Isn't this a great colour?"

And then he leaned over and kissed me, finally, after

years as competitors, as collaborators, as friends closer than family. Everyone had assumed we were coupled, but he'd never kissed me before. And I'd followed his lead, drawn by him wherever he was going.

As we kissed, he touched my face, my shoulder, my hair. When he pulled back, I sat a while with my eyes closed. Sunshine is a preservative.

That's how it began. And I thought it would go on forever.

A year later, when we were both at Queen's, he stopped sleeping in our bed and moved a few short feet—just beyond the bedroom wall, in fact—to sleep with our roommate, Sandra. I couldn't afford to move out, having made no other friends, so I couldn't escape the drama. When they made love, she alternated whimpers and screams. When they fought, she screamed even louder and smashed things, usually against the shared bedroom wall.

After one particularly stormy night—I think they were fighting, but I was beyond caring—I decamped to the lumpy, stained couch in the living room. Ricky came out of the bedroom on the way to the bathroom and stopped when he saw me.

I think he tried to say something.

I think it was "I'm sorry."

I had closed my eyes and put my hands over my ears.

"Young love," people said when they found out we had broken up. "It happens."

Other people. They said it.

I was never comfortable at university after that, and then I met Roger at a club and followed him back to Ohio. No goodbye to Rick.

But for several years, in the juicy freshness of spring, I thought of him and that day at The Bluffs, and I tried to forget the way we ended.

I fire a question into the silence: "Why a motorcycle?"

He looks out at the water and shrugs. "Dunno. It felt

right."

It felt right? I want to roll my eyes but I am polite. "What kind is it? I don't know why I'm even asking. Harley-Davidson is the only one I know."

He laughs with a snort that indicates disgust at Harleys but somehow doesn't make me feel stupid. "She's an Aprilia. A strong company before World War II, out of business in the early 50s, back in the late 90s, went bankrupt again, et cetera. Anyway, mine's not antique. A Stasera, from 2001."

"It's very pretty." I have noticed the gleaming red and cream, and the studs on the leather seats and across the bags on the back. "In a tough-guy way, of course."

"Like the company says, 'Powerful works of art.'" He leans on his forearms, hands folded together, looking ahead. "I do love the power." Pause. "And the speed."

"Adrenaline junkie?" I tease.

He smiles at me before turning back to the water. "A little. It's like flying, overcoming the pull of the earth holding me down. Plus," he hesitates, "when I got sober, I needed something to get absorbed in. Something besides public policy or words. Now I run and lift weights, and I ride my motorcycle."

Sober? "Why don't I make some coffee?"

I head into the kitchen, fighting the urge to hide my wineglass. I grind beans and fill the coffeemaker's water reservoir, swigging wine. I push "on" and rejoin him on the deck, leaving my glass in the kitchen. He's sitting in a plastic recliner, hands behind his head, black boots crossed at the ankle. I stand facing the house, my elbows on the deck rail.

He gestures toward the moon. "God, look at that. Just a slice can still cast a huge trail on the water. I'd forgotten how arresting it is."

"Sometimes at this time of year, when there's just a little haze and a full moon, it's light enough out here to read past midnight." He's silent. I fidget. "The moon rises

183

in Toronto, surely?"

"Yeah, but you can't see the moon for the lights. Cliché but true." He yawns.

I turn sideways and look out. "Well, the full moon itself is cliché. I like all the phases. They leave room for the imagination."

"Not so much left to imagine anymore. We don't remember a time before the Americans walked on it. And now Japan has mapped the entire surface. Even the dark side."

I had read this factoid to Daddy from one of the magazines. "Maps are okay. They're not the same as knowing a place yourself, though. They give you an outline, but they're limited—you know, here be dragons and all."

For the first time, Ricky really looks at me and his smile reaches his eyes. "That's true."

My cheeks feel hot—from Ricky's approval? From embarrassment at needing it?

He blinks and looks away. "I've found that on my bike, too. On a map, there's a dot and a name, and you think it's a city. But on the Lake Superior northeast shore, it's probably a boarded-up A&W and an abandoned motel."

I blurt, "Yeah, reality doesn't always match imagination. There's that Japanese concept, the beauty in imperfection? What's it called...all I can think of is hara kiri and I know that's not it." I need to stop babbling.

"Wabi sabi." Rick says it flatly. "I read it a lot. Apparently, it's necessary in badly written artist statements."

"Yes, that's it. My niece was talking about it when she was here." Rick shows no signs of asking, so I fill in, "That's Victoria, Marilyn's daughter—you remember, she was born just before we started at Queen's. She's almost done her MFA, if you can believe that. Where'd the time go?"

He nods. More silence.

This time, I force myself to wait it out. Shouldn't he say something? Like, now that we're talking about Queen's and long ago, he could say how sorry he is for dumping me. Young love...it happens. Will he even mention my father? I turn away from him, searching the moon.

Behind me, I hear him yawn again. I press my lips together to keep from asking, Am I boring you? I pretend the coffee needs attention.

Once inside, I Google Ricky, which I actually had considered but had avoided to keep from ruining my fantasy. A "Richard M. Johnson" is a consultant in arts policy analysis and speechwriting, having left behind some job with the province I don't recognize.

Still, "consultant" can mean anything, right? Before Daddy's illness, I managed a large insurance company. The administrative function. In the home office. The reception desk. Fine, I answered phones and handed out brochures and made coffee. For Roger and his father and his cousin, all partners in the family business. Whatever.

Coffee. I pour two mugs and put them onto a small tray with sugar and milk and spoons. Out on the deck, I set down the tray. He sweetens a mug and lifts it toward the newly visible stars.

"How's your astronomy these days?" He laughs, adding, "I never learned anything beyond the Big Dipper. Ursa Major, right?"

"That's not really a constellation. It's just a star pattern, an asterism." I hear how flat my voice is, without the humour I meant to include.

He raises an eyebrow. "Really? And who decides these things, anyway?"

He sounds amused, but in case he's annoyed, I lighten my tone. "Some official group of star deciders, I guess."

"There'd be a job to have."

In silence, we drink coffee.

Rick clears his throat. "Map or no map, it's pretty. Hard to believe that anything that beautiful is just a sterile

185

rock."

"Not necessarily. There might be water bears out there. Ursa Aqua, as it were."

Rick looks at me, puzzled, and I show off.

"Tardigrades. Related to sea monkeys. Known as water bears or moss piglets. They go dormant in dry conditions. The Europeans sent some into space and brought 'em home. When they added water, the tardigrades start reproducing. Survived the radiation and everything. So they, or something like them, could be out there right now. Just dormant."

Rick blinks.

I smile. "Modern dragons, eh. Sorry to add them to the terrible map that takes all the mystery out of everything."

And then I don't give him any more chances. Instead, I talk about going through the house, everything my parents kept, how Marilyn and I have a lot to do. Nothing important—nothing I couldn't have said to the people who'd gathered in the kitchen after my father's death.

Out of the corner of my eye, I see Rick drain his mug and set it down. He looks at his fingernails.

I hum, "The world is full of light." I'm done with wine and procrastination. Tomorrow, I'll grow up. Really start in on this house, for Marilyn's sake. Call my husband, though I don't quite know what I'll say.

"That's okay," my father tells me. "Just start, for Chrissake."

As Rick and I thread our way through the living room, I realize I'm not sure who made the first move. Who's leaving whom.

Waiting politely on the porch while Rick fastens his helmet, I hug myself. I think of my father but I'm neither sentimental enough nor still drunk enough to yell and flap my arms, like our goose. Instead, as the roar of the motorcycle fades, I snap off the porch light and blow a kiss to the tardigrades on the moon.

ABOUT THE AUTHORS

DONNA QUICK

I was a features writer at a daily newspaper for several years. My pre-retirement job was 21 years as a copy editor for a government publication. I've won three magazine fiction contests and a dozen medals in the Alberta 55 Plus Seniors Games creative writing competitions. I've had articles published in Our Canada, Canadian Cowboy Country, Western Producer, Rural Heritage (U.S.), the Edmonton Journal, and a number of regional publications.

MAUREEN O'HARE

Maureen O'Hare dabbles in all forms of art. She draws, paints and carves with special interest in fantasy images. She reads incessantly while conveniently providing a comfortable lap for her very demanding cat. Her other forms of entertainment include punching tiny holes in targets with her recurve bow and arrows.

MICHELE LISIECKI

I'm a middle school teacher in my eighteenth year of teaching. I've studied under Robert J. Sawyer, David B. Coe, and Faith Hunter, I am a member of the Imaginative Fiction Writers Association, and I'm on the committee for When Words Collide.

MICHAEL LALONDE

I was a semifinalist in the 2013 John Kenneth Galbraith Literary Award. My writing has appeared in the online magazine /I & Eye,/ /The Prairie Journal/, and the summer 2016 issue of /Island Writer/ magazine. Visit my website: www.mikelalonde.com

MAUREEN HASELOH

Maureen Haseloh is a writer. After she finished her BA in English, she worked at various jobs until becoming a Hospital Unit Clerk. She enjoys writing, working in a hospital and managing her husband's business. She lives with her husband, daughter and four cats.

ALLISON GORNER

Allison Gorner graduated from the Southern Alberta Institute of Technology (S.A.I.T.) with a diploma in Cinema, Television, Stage and Radio. She majored as writer/director for television and has always loved to create stories. She grew up in the Rocky Mountains of British Columbia and spent her time reading, biking, playing sports, and hiking. She lives in Pincher Creek, Alberta with her husband and four children.

JOAN M. BARIL

Joan M. Baril, is a short story writer who has had fifty-three fiction and nonfiction pieces published in literary magazines including Prairie Fire, Room, Northword, Anitgonish Review, Other Voices, CanadianWomen's Studies, Canadian Forum, Herizons, Ten Stories High, The New Orphic Review. She won several awards for her work including taking first place for short fiction in 2015 and 2016 in the North-western Ontario Writers annual contest. Her story, "The Yegg Boy' was nominated for the Journey Prize by the Antigonish Review.

For several years, her columns on women's and immigrant issues appeared in the Thunder Bay Post and Northern Woman's Journal. In 1992 the Canadian government honoured her for her work with immigrants and for her column on immigrant issues. She has published articles in national magazines mainly Herizons and Canadian Forumn.

She blogs at Literary Thunder Bay.

SARA MANG

I am a new writer and am currently enrolled in the Creative Writing program at the University of British Columbia. Originally from Labrador, I was an artillery officer in the Canadian Forces before retiring in 2011 to be at home with my three children. I am currently working on a collection of short stories.

WAYNE DOUGLAS WEEDON

I have been writing for over sixty years. I have a portfolio of three novels, many short stories, poetry, and numerous pieces of non-fiction.

Besides a novel, Free To Think, available at

http://www.friesenpress.com/bookstore/title/119734000010981281/Wayne-Douglas-Weedon-Free-To-Think, on Amazon, or your local bookstore, I have published short stories and non-fiction in "Lifestyles 55", "Smartbiz", "HAAM Magazine" and "Lennox, The Magazine". At age sixty-five, I retired and became a full-time student at the University of Winnipeg. This past June, I graduated with a Bachelor of Arts majoring in English. At university, besides Creative Writing, I have taken subjects that have always interested me, which included: Religion, Philosophy, Anthropology, Investigative Journalism, Rhetoric and Theatre.

Although I write poetry and non-fiction, most of my work is fiction based on real life, which includes: my experiences, things I have read, as well as stories told to me by others.

VICKI LOCKWOOD
Vicki lives in the Rocky Mountains of Alberta where she is inspired by the natural beauty of the area. She likes to write stories that invoke an emotional connection with her characters who have various incidents and encounters with and in their Canadian surroundings.

R.O.
R.O. lives in Northern Ontario, tucked away between here and there, with an extraordinarily 'almost human' dog. Gathering inspiration from daily life and historical events, R.O's work often depicts Canadian themes centred around diversity, and equality. As an active supporter and collector of Canadian music and art, R.O enjoys sharing the joy of Canadian culture with others.

MARION AGNEW
After fifteen years as a technical writer and editor, Marion Agnew moved to Thunder Bay, Ontario. Her fiction and nonfiction have appeared in journals such as Prairie Fire, The Malahat Review, Room, New Orphic Review, South Dakota Review, and Compose, and have been selected for the Ten Stories High anthology (11th, 15th, and 17th editions) and Best Canadian Essays (2012 and 2014). She writes from her home office in Shuniah, just outside Thunder Bay, overlooking Lake Superior. More information at www.marionagnew.ca

71464832R00124

Made in the USA
Columbia, SC
28 May 2017